THE
VALENTINE
SUITE

The Valentine Suite

By

Tracy Broemmer

Women's Fiction

Published by Tracy Broemmer

Edited by Lexie Broemmer

Cover Photo: Deposit Photos

Cover Design: Vanilla Lily Designs

ISBN#: 978-1-951637-34-7

I plotted this book in the summer of 2019, after my laptop was stolen and I lost 17 chapters of work on 2 different projects. I was broken for many reasons that year. In August of 2019, JB and I spent a few days in an absolutely beautiful suite in a beach property in California. I managed to hammer out 18K words on a manuscript I started after losing so much in the spring. And I plotted this one, knowing some day I would come back to it.

Although this book has nothing to do with Alzheimer's Disease, I was grieving my mother when I plotted Alys & Fletch's story. She passed away in 2020, but we started losing her in 2014. This book let me channel all the darkness, fear, and grief into something productive.

So maybe this book is for all the beautiful places in the world that somehow heal our hearts or at least begin the healing process.

Praise for The Valentine Suite

Is it possible to reassemble the pieces of a shattered life?

Recently divorced and emotionally devastated from too many losses, Alys Holland has one week to kick back and relax before friends and family arrive at the posh resort for her son's wedding. But when her ex-husband, Fletcher, unlocks the door to her resort suite and walks right in, Alys knows that nothing about this week is going to be relaxing.

This moment sets the stage for an emotional rollercoaster that had me near tears for the entire story.

The novel is filled with a likable, solid cast of characters, several that I'd love to hear more about. The setting—a beautiful oceanfront resort—stands in complete opposition to the pain that Alys has suffered. At first, the roil of the ocean waves holds Alys's attention more than anything, but as the story progresses, she seems to notice the perfectly maintained grounds and the abundance of flowers, indicating the beginning steps to healing her broken heart.

The Valentine Suite by Tracy Broemmer is an excellent example of women's fiction. While this novel is written exclusively from Alys Holland's point of view, the reader is not privy to all of her heartache up front. Ms. Broemmer has a way of twisting and turning through the plot, slowly peeling away the layers of backstory to reveal the secrets and heart-wrenching sorrow that brought her characters to the breaking point.

If you enjoy an emotional read about finding a small piece of happiness within the ruins, *The Valentine Suite* is the perfect novel for you. –Kate Carley, author of *Changing Krysset Series*

"...*The Valentine Suite* is an achingly beautiful and emotional glimpse of how grief can shatter souls and love can be a healing salvation..." —Tonya Mathenia, *InD'Tale Magazine*

About The Valentine Suite

Some love stories don't end—they just break.

Two years after losing two of their children in a tragic accident, Alys and Fletcher Holland are no longer a couple, barely even speaking. But their son's destination wedding forces a reunion neither of them wants.

Alys plans to keep her distance, endure the festivities, and escape back to her quiet, controlled life. But when a booking mix-up puts her and Fletch in the Valentine Suite, close quarters make it impossible to ignore the man she loved for over twenty-five years.

Fletch still frustrates her. Still protects her. And with every stolen moment, every unspoken truth, the cracks in their broken hearts start to mend.

Will their stay in paradise be enough to bring their family back together—or prove they were always meant to stay apart?

A heart-wrenching, family drama about love, loss, and finding your way back.

Chapter One

FRIDAY, AUGUST 9, 2019

She sipped her bourbon by the light of the moon on the Pacific. The invitation—studied for the hundredth time—on the small wicker table at her side was forgotten for the moment. She should be thinking about Ledger, about Ledger and Brooke, but she couldn't. Not now. Not here.

Alys Holland rested her head on the lounge chair and closed her eyes only to open them immediately. She'd only just arrived in Palos Verdes earlier in the evening—after a four-hour flight, a thirty-four-minute wait at the rental car counter, and a quick stop at a liquor store in Redondo Beach. The next two weeks that stretched out before her beckoned, invited relaxation, respite, healing. The trouble with that being that she would need to tear the scars away and dig into the pain to heal completely.

She wasn't willing to do that. Not for Iva. Not for Fletch or Claire.

Not even for Ledger.

Still, her chest felt squeezed, painfully so. Gasping to breathe, Alys leaned forward, coughing hard at the tightening sensation. Shoulder and neck pain were sometimes symptoms of a heart attack in women; she had read somewhere that coughing could save someone suffering a heart attack until help arrived.

She wasn't having a heart attack, though. If Iva were here, she would tell her that. She would roll her blue eyes and laugh at Alys, though usually Alys laughed, too, and laughing together took the sting out of Iva's words.

No heart attack, though at her lowest points—and there had been so many now—she would have welcomed it. Death, sure. If there was a god, Alys would have died two years ago. The fact that she hadn't, that she still woke in a comfortable bed every day, was why she quit believing. She would take death, gladly, and she would take the horrible pain and die in the most horrible way possible.

If only.

She heard music in the distance. Someone trying to sing an old Foreigner song, though the voice most definitely did not belong to Lou Gramm. Was it still the same band who had played at the bar two years ago?

The bar—Howie's, no use pretending she didn't remember the name—was just north of the main hotel where she was now. Where she and Fletch had stayed then. Still part of the resort campus, it was a family friendly bar and grill, and when they had wandered there, hand in hand one night, there was a summer festival going on. Perfect for enjoying live music and cold beer while you waited for a table.

She and Fletch had grabbed a beer—Fletch was into weird IPAs at the time and he had ordered a Firestone Walker Mind

Haze, while teasing her about her simple, safe lager—and wandered over to the fence to watch the sunset bleed dark purple and a deep, flushed pink over the ocean, already black with night.

Alys thought the music was mediocre, but mostly, she remembered that incredible sunset and the feel of Fletch's warm, solid body at her side.

She sipped from her thick glass tumbler. The glasses —*everything*—here was nicer than her own personal belongings. Which was saying something, because she and Fletch had done well together, and they had amassed a lot of nice things.

Lost some, too.

Without meaning to, she rubbed her thumb over the underside of her ring finger. That ring had been gone for over two years, but there were still times when she found herself checking for it. One time, she had actually panicked when she didn't find it, when she had found her ring finger bare. Thankfully, since she had taken the ring off, she was usually alone, and no one was there to witness her near breakdown.

Well, Iva had seen the breakdowns, but Alys was grateful she hadn't seen *that* one. Iva wouldn't have blinked; she would have talked her through it. Held her. Let her scream and cry. Whatever it took. Just the way Iva was put together. So generous. Selfless.

The knot of emotion in her throat was almost welcome. Except it was wrong that she could cry for Iva and nothing else. She rested her head on the chair again and closed her eyes. Over the past couple of years, she had become good at being cold. At boxing up the heartache and shoving it to the back of her mind. It was the only way she had survived.

Well, that and Iva. But again, even Alys knew that was wrong.

A gentle wind lifted a wispy curl of hair from her shoulder. She felt it on her cheek, but she didn't move to brush it away. The glass in her hand was heavy enough to keep her weighted in the present, so she let her mind tiptoe back to the past and look at the mess.

Ledger deserved more than this. More from her.

The Valentine Suite.

She and Fletch had stayed here for their twenty-fifth anniversary. By some insane luck, they'd been given the suite, and for the first twenty-four hours, they hadn't left it. They hadn't left the king-sized bed. Hadn't spent more than five minutes apart, skin to skin even when they stopped for coffee or breakfast or room service dinners.

They had laughed.

She and Fletch had laughed so much together through the years, but on that trip, they'd laughed off the whispers of the housekeeping staff. Alys had overheard them—two ladies, one probably a few years older than Alys and the other several years younger—whispering and sharing rumors in little singsong voices. No one who stayed overnight in The Valentine Suite stayed together. Alys had no idea how they would know such a thing, but the idea that she and Fletch would ever be separated was enough to make the two of them laugh.

They were separated and divorced within the year.

That heartache was just as raw as the rest of it, so she never allowed herself to look back.

Fletch had moved on. In fact, Brooke had said something once about Trish, his plus one, and then she'd turned seven shades of red, horrified that she'd said something like that in front of Alys. Alys had simply nodded, because if Iva were still around, she would probably have brought her to the wedding.

She didn't even know Ledger anymore. She'd given birth to him twenty-four years ago—he and Jade—and she'd lost him as surely as she lost Jade. And Kase. Maybe losing Ledger was her fault, but he was better off without her. She couldn't see him through the grief, and no son deserved a mother who was blind to his face, to his heart. He had Fletch, still. And Claire.

And Brooke.

Alys wasn't sure what she thought about Brooke. The girl was beautiful, no question. Of course, the long-legged, slender blonde had drawn Ledger's attention. She was smart; Alys knew she was in nursing at the local hospital. What she didn't know was what the sound of her laugh did to her son. If they held hands when they walked through the grocery store. If Brooke wanted a family or how she would feel if Ledger didn't.

Because Alys wouldn't want a family if she were Ledger. No way in hell. Family invited passion and pain and gut-wrenching grief.

At the sound of the heavy door of the suite banging closed, she opened her eyes. Housekeeping? She'd forgotten to tell them she didn't need the bed turned down. No need for anything romantic, no need for anything at all. She might have forgotten how to feel, but she was functional. She could pull the fluffy white comforter back, plump her own pillows, and turn down the lights.

Maybe if she was quiet, the housekeeper wouldn't even realize she was there. Which would be fine. Alys was perfectly capable of getting by. Her professional self had thrived after her heart stopped, but she had no use for small talk.

She rested her head on the chair again and fixed her gaze on the Pacific and found herself thinking of Virginia Woolf. She imagined filling her coat pockets with heavy stones and walking into the ocean. No stopping. No looking back.

No regrets.

Well. There would always be regrets.

She heard footsteps behind her. The sound of something rolling or coasting. Mesmerized by the dulled roar of the ocean waves, she ignored the sounds. Maybe they'd brought room service, though she hadn't ordered anything. She'd forced herself to eat trail mix on the flight. The bourbon in her glass now was all she needed.

"Allie?"

Fletcher's voice was low and gritty, and so out of place here, for just a moment, she tried to tell herself she was hearing things. She wasn't, though. She could feel him behind her now. His heavy gaze at her back. That electric charge around them that always seemed to tether them together. Funny that they'd been divorced for a while now and she could still feel that instinctual connection to him.

"What're you doing here?"

His words chased chills over her arms, but she refused to give in and rub them away. She wouldn't let him see that he had any effect on her. Instead, she squeezed her eyes closed and wished him away. Anywhere but here.

Well, not anywhere. Although if she could wish him gone and bring back Jade or Kase...

"What am I doing here?" Her whisper was thick with exhaustion and bourbon and some of that regret, though she would deny it if Fletch called her on it. "Really, Fletch?"

"Really, Alys." He joined her on the balcony now. Hands in the hip pockets of his navy trousers, he sauntered past her without looking at her and stood at the rail of the balcony.

"You know what I'm doing here," she said quietly. "And I'm not up for games."

"Why are you in this suite?"

"Because I called and booked it several months ago for the wedding." Head still on the chair, she pulled in a long, deep breath and stared at the fancy cut crystal glass in her hand.

"So did I."

Behind the glass, Fletch turned toward her. She fought the urge to look, to really look at him, but as always, he won that fight. With just her eyes, she noticed his right hand still tucked in his pocket, but he rested his left hand on the rail. She stared for a moment at his bare fingers, wondering what he had done with his wedding band. Had he sold it? Doubtful. It was worthless, and anyway, Fletch wasn't the type to sell a valuable baseball card. Not because he needed *things*, but more because he didn't take the time to care. He didn't need money.

Had he thrown it in the back of a dresser drawer?

"That's impossible," she mumbled, eyes still on his hand. She blinked to clear away the mental image of sliding that band onto his finger over twenty-five years ago. The sincerity in his eyes and the ornery grin he'd flashed at her before they turned back to Father Cole.

"I booked before Thanksgiving," he argued.

She'd booked the room before Halloween, but she didn't want to waste a peaceful evening fighting with Fletcher.

"Where's Trixie?"

She hated that she asked, but on the other hand, she didn't want to be blindsided when the girl suddenly appeared on the balcony with Fletch. She hated that her childish, irrational jealousy had reared its head and called his girlfriend Trixie, because Alys knew damned well it wasn't her name.

Mostly, she hated that her voice broke the slightest bit when she said her name, and judging from the pained look on Fletch's face, he noticed. Alys flicked her eyes up to meet his, but the heat in his gaze made her uncomfortable. Once, she had loved his intense nature. Now she had no patience for it.

"Trish," he corrected her. Alys dipped her eyes down to his broad shoulders as he shrugged and shook his head. "She's not coming."

"What do you mean she's not coming? Brooke said you were bringing her." Alys knocked back the last of the bourbon. She eyed the tumbler with regret and then scooted forward to the end of the lounge chair.

"Well, she's not." He shrugged and turned his back to her again.

"I booked the suite before Halloween, Fletch," she mumbled as she stood and slipped back through the sliding doors.

"Did you book it under Alys Holland?" he called.

"What other name would I use?" She made her way through the heavily shadowed living area to take her glass to the kitchenette. Five minutes ago, she'd been content. Certain she could get through the next two weeks unaffected and go back to her life as usual. What was left of it. Five minutes with Fletch and she felt like her skin was on too tight.

She eyed the bottle of High West as she bumped the faucet on to rinse her glass out.

"Maybe they still had us in their computer."

With a sigh and a silent plea to someone other than the god she didn't believe in, Alys set the glass on the counter and reached for the bottle. She poured more whiskey with a steady hand and listened to the staccato footsteps of Fletch's loafers cross through the dining room. The bark of a chair on the floor made her jump. Fletcher muttered something and then, even with her back to the door, she knew he was there behind her again.

"Maybe they just thought we were..."

She drank when he hesitated and ducked her head over the glass.

"Still..."

"Whatever, Fletch." She shrugged. "We can't both stay here."

"I'll take care of it in the morning."

"In the morning?" She whirled around to look at him. The sight of him, head bent and fingers pinching the bridge of his nose, squeezed her heart. "Take care of it now. We're not sleeping together."

"It's after midnight, Allie. I'm beat." He dropped his hand to his side and eyed her in the shadows. "I'll sleep on the couch."

"The couch?" She laughed. "You're not gonna fit on the couch."

"Well, that's my problem, isn't it?"

She held the eye contact, but in the darkness, she couldn't read his face to know what he was thinking. With another sigh, she drank the last of the whiskey in her glass and then rinsed it.

"Do you do that a lot?" His voice was gruff.

"Do what?" She capped the bottle and then stepped to the door to leave the room.

"Drink alone."

He dragged his gaze down her front. In the absence of light, she felt it linger on her breasts and her hips. Feeling exposed now, she shifted her bare feet and wished she hadn't changed into the sleep shorts when she'd arrived earlier. At least she still wore her blouse and her bra. There was no way Fletch could see the way his intense stare affected her, but he knew her well enough to imagine.

"No one to drink with, Fletch," she whispered.

"Allie." The hurt in his voice drove her from the room. Her bare leg brushed his trousers as she hurried out. "Goddammit, that's not—"

"Just don't." She spoke so quietly, it was a wonder he heard her. Alys shot a glance at the couches he had alluded to moments ago. Fletch was a tall guy with broad shoulders and powerful thighs. He wouldn't fit on the damned couches. Not to mention, they might be comfortable for sitting in front of the TV for a short time, but they weren't made for overnight sleeping. He would sleep better on ballpark bleachers.

He followed her into the hall, but when she felt him come up short behind her, she turned to look at him. Hands propped on his hips, he stared at the bed. The same bed they'd shared when they had come to celebrate their anniversary.

"I'll find something else," he mumbled.

"Yeah?" She tipped her head. "What're you gonna find at this hour?"

"I don't know," he admitted. "But I'm not gonna stand here and fight with you. It's been a hell of a day. This is the last thing I need."

A mix of anger and guilt ripped through her.

"Fletch."

"I'll sleep in the rental car," he mumbled. "And get this straightened out in the morning."

"You can't sleep in the car," she argued.

"It couldn't be any worse than the couch."

Irritated by the sting of tears, she threw her hands up and stepped into the bathroom. Bright lights around the mirror highlighted the age in her skin, the wrinkles around her eyes. She'd left the lamp on in the bedroom, so she could navigate through the suite to come to bed, but she hated the bright lights in here.

"You don't have to do that," she said to her reflection. Fletch propped himself in the doorway and folded his arms over his chest.

"No? So, what do you suggest we do?"

"Just stay here tonight and figure it out in the morning." She kept her gaze averted as she reached for her toothbrush.

"Allie—"

"You can sleep in the bed." She swallowed hard.

"You sure?"

She shrugged and nodded, but she still refused to meet his eyes. Seeing her reflection was a reminder. There was nothing left between her and Fletch; there was nothing left of herself. She was kidding herself if she thought he couldn't make it through a night in a bed beside her and keep his hands to himself.

Chapter Two

THEY SLEPT WITH THE BALCONY DOOR OPEN, THE same as they did when they had come to celebrate their anniversary. There hadn't been much sleep that night in the past, and Alys hadn't slept much last night, either, but for different reasons. She had lain awake most of the night, hugging her side of the bed, as if Fletch wouldn't be able to keep his hands off her.

Laughable, because she couldn't remember the last time they had made love.

She awoke to the smell of coffee and the sound of shower water pattering on the tiled walls. For just a moment, she lay with her eyes closed and listened. The rolling ocean outside their room spoke to her. Today she would venture out for a walk. Alys stretched and allowed herself a small thrill at the feel of the crisp, cool sheet on her bare legs. She imagined Fletch in the shower, water pelting his broad shoulders. Small drops rolling over his chest and the flat plain of his stomach. The tangle of dark hair that narrowed at his waist.

They had gone to Cabo a few years before the divorce, and Alys had surprised him with a French bikini wax. He'd loved it, and he had suggested she pierce her nipples or get a tattoo. Alys had only laughed and suggested he go in for a Brazilian ball wax, knowing that would shut him up.

The thought of him nude right now stirred a longing buried deep in her belly.

"Jesus." She snapped at herself and jack knifed in the king-sized bed. Most definitely not going there.

When they were younger, when the kids were very little, Fletch sang in the shower. Goofy songs—anything from "Itsy Bitsy Teeny Weeny Yellow Polka Dot Bikini" to "Pink Shoelaces" because sometimes the boys showered with him, and a few times Jade had wandered in and out of the bathroom. Alys didn't strain to hear him singing now; life had leached the joy out of both of them, and she doubted her ex-husband would remember the tune of a fun song, let alone the lyrics.

With a deep sigh, she threw off the top sheet and the fluffy white comforter and swung her legs around to sit on the side of the bed. Hers was the side that faced the balcony, the ocean. That didn't matter so much today as having her back to Fletch did.

She hated mornings, because for a long time, she had hoped to not wake up with the next sunrise. Iva used to watch her with those intense damned eyes that saw everything, and mornings were particularly hard. Iva would brush her shoulder with her fingertips as she passed her a cup of coffee. Alys tried hard not to, but inevitably, she would look up and meet Iva's eyes and know what she was thinking.

Sympathy. Empathy, even.

Never pity.

She needed coffee, even if Fletch had made it. The bourbon from last night pounded now in her head and rattled her brain. She'd gone back for more after Fletch had brushed his teeth, stripped down to his boxers, and fallen in bed. True to form, he had been asleep the second his head hit the pillow, and the heat of his body all the way across the king-sized mattress had driven Alys back to the kitchenette.

Why hadn't Trish come with him?

Alys gave herself a mental shake. Not her business. Nothing about Fletcher Holland was her business anymore. The buzz of her cell phone drew her attention to the glass-topped white wicker nightstand. A calendar reminder flashed on the screen, but she was more interested in the steaming white mug beside her phone.

Fletch had brought her coffee before getting in the shower.

With a muttered curse, she planted her hands in the mattress and shoved upward to stand. She didn't want or need him to do things for her. Nice things. Even if they were simple. Even if it meant nothing. She had two healthy legs, and she was capable of walking to the kitchenette to pour her own coffee.

At her suitcase, she groped for a sports bra and yoga pants, eyes on the closed bathroom door. When they were here for their anniversary, they had made good use of that extra big shower. Fingers catching in the strap of a bra, Alys looked back at the suitcase, tugged the black bra and her black pants out and retreated to the bedroom. She closed the door and tossed the clothes on the bed.

Dammit all, the coffee smelled so good.

He wouldn't have to know she took a sip. Eyes on the slice of daylight in the slit of the drapes, Alys wound her way around the foot of the bed and stopped when she found herself toed up against the leg of the nightstand. Ignoring the slight tremble in her hand, she picked the mug up and lifted it to her face. Before drinking it, she breathed deeply and inhaled the strong, almost nutty, aroma.

Memories flashed—Ledger missing a front tooth, grinning at her over a bowl of Cheerios. Jade sipping coffee, eyes on her biology text. Fletch backed up against the kitchen counter, bare feet crossed at the ankles, his fingers curled around the black Darth Vader mug the kids had given him for Father's Day several years ago.

Alys gulped the hot liquid, preferring the scald on her tongue and her throat to the horrid stab of pain the memories brought. Another swallow calmed the vicious grief the memories always dragged with them. She eyed the closed door, set the mug down in such a rush coffee sloshed over the top and splashed the screen of her phone, and then hurried back around the bed.

She eyed her bare fingernails as she locked the door for good measure. Fletch wasn't going to walk in on her, not on purpose. Still, she whipped her tank off and yanked the sports bra over her head as quickly as she could. Never mind the memories, the laughter, that brought back. She and Fletch walking the ocean front path the last time they were here. She and Fletch running for the memory walk for their local Alzheimer's office. Fletch trying to help her tug the sweat-soaked sports bra up over her damp skin and her head so she could shower and get Jade to her piano lesson.

Shedding the sleep shorts, she swiped the yoga pants from the foot of the bed and danced around to tug them on. She'd lost weight, and the damned things sagged like the pantyhose her mother had insisted she wear when she was inducted into the honor society in high school. She should replace them, but really, she couldn't be bothered to shop.

Buying stuff for this trip had been an ordeal, from the damned mother-of-the-groom dress to the travel size deodorant. She'd shopped enough in the past month for the next few years, and she would be happy to rot in the house Iva had left her, even if it meant someone would find her dead body dressed in worn, faded, and stained pants and a sports bra that no longer had the elastic fortitude to hold her sagging breasts up.

In a hurry now to get out before Fletch did—she should be so lucky as to only have to see him at the wedding—Alys dropped to sit on the edge of the bed and reached for her running shoes. Only to remember she needed socks. The shower water had stopped, but lost in the memories she pretended meant no more than random glimpses of a TV screen, she hadn't paid attention.

Now the closed French door rattled. Alys squeezed her eyes closed when she heard Fletch's muttered curse. Because she needed socks, and not because she felt bad for locking him out, she stood and opened the door and squeezed past him, ignoring his continued cursing.

"You really needed to lock me out?"

When they were married, Fletch wore Dior Sauvage, and there were times Alys couldn't keep her hands off him. Today he wore something different, and even though it smelled just about as delicious on him, the scent and irrational anger nearly choked her. She met his eyes for a second and looked away, wondering if Trish had coaxed him to change his signature scent.

Did they shower together the way she and Fletch had when they were married? Finish each other's sentences? Did Trish hover over his shoulder and try to help him do the crossword puzzle in the Sunday paper the way Alys used to?

"I'm going for a walk," she announced, chin on her chest as she dug through her luggage again, this time for socks.

"Have you seen Ledger yet?" Fletch's voice was gruff.

"They're not here yet."

Truth was she hadn't seen Ledger in several months.

"Claire?"

Perched on the gray padded bench at the foot of the bed, Alys put her socks on and then worked her feet into her shoes. She hadn't seen Claire, either. The thought nearly made her throw up a little bit in her mouth.

"I got in late last night, Fletch." She sounded snippy, even to herself. She tied her shoes quickly and shot up from the bench. Fletch watched her snatch her phone from the nightstand. She noticed when he glanced at the mug of coffee that was largely untouched. His face was blank when she looked at him.

"She's looking forward to seeing you."

Alys tucked her phone into the pocket of her pants and mentally searched her cosmetics bag. She hoped she had remembered her antacids. Seeing Claire might be harder than seeing Fletch and Ledger. She chose to ignore his announcement; why would he even say that anyway?

"Sure as hell don't know why."

Her shoulders tightened at his parting words. She paused, considered snapping back at him. No point in it, though. She probably deserved it and more. Besides, walking away without arguing would get under Fletch's skin ten times deeper than anything she could say.

Claire Delaney used to call her every day. When she didn't, Alys made the call. They talked about everything from their babies teething to the cost of a gallon of milk to earth-shattering orgasms to the best way to prepare dressing for Thanksgiving dinner. They'd shared engagement news and weddings and the death of parents, and they'd shared laughter and hangovers and stomach flus and tears.

Alys had loved her. As much as she loved Fletch, but in a completely different way, of course.

She'd loved her. Until she didn't.

The thought of seeing her now chased the black coffee Fletch had made back up her throat. Dr. Rabie had prescribed something for the acid reflux, but Alys being Alys, she never bothered to fill the prescription. Instead, now and then— when she needed to—she popped a generic over the counter antacid. And she'd only bought those because the bottle of Tums she had in her cabinet were old and stale.

With two weeks until the wedding, a week until any wedding festivities started, Claire and Josh wouldn't be here yet, would they? Seemed impossible that the two of them could get two weeks off at the same time when they used to struggle to get away for a long weekend. Claire's position in HR at The Grove kept her busier than she liked, and Josh was gone on business for weeks at a time. No way either of them were in Palos Verdes yet. Fletch had been messing with her.

Unless.

A wedding was a big thing. Something to plan a big vacation around. Ledger and Brooke had sent out save the date cards a good six to eight months ago, so anyone and everyone had time to get time off and stick some money away for a prolonged vacation.

Worried now that Claire would appear in the hall as she made her way to the lobby, Alys slowed her steps. A whirl of yellow and orange sashayed around the corner, causing her to startle. She nearly jumped backwards. The woman in the bright floral caftan hummed as she walked. She shot a curious look at Alys but kept going without comment. Alys ran her fingers through her shaggy hair, wishing she had grabbed her ballcap and sunglasses.

She snorted and shook her head as she rounded yet another corner and passed a brightly lit display case that showcased high-end items like Tom Ford sunglasses and a pair of Manolo Blahnik floral pumps. Pushing the memory of her own Manolo Blahniks from her mind—blue pointed-toe pumps from the days before she changed her wardrobe to nearly all black—she hurried through the lobby, avoiding eye contact with anyone as she burst out the glass doors that led to the courtyard out back.

A cool breeze chased her down the brick stairs to the walking path that led around the resort campus. With a shiver, she lifted a hand to shield her eyes and looked up, searching for the sun. Weak rays fell behind clouds; the sun itself partially hidden. It was early yet; Alys glanced at her watch as she skipped down the last of the stairs. She was shocked to find it was after eight. Fletch was usually up and out the door by six in the mornings.

Odds were, by midmorning, the clouds would clear out. She took a right on the path and stretched her arms over her head as she headed north up the path. To her left, the ocean stretched and rolled a deep blue. The campus of the Kahalina Bluff Resort sprawled over several square miles to the right. Vivid, riotous colors dotted the resort grounds, where flowers were planted either right in the earth or in barrels and other shaped planters.

Growing up, Alys had only known what roses and tulips were, but when she and Fletch built the house on Emery Court, they'd commissioned landscapers to plant trees and flower beds. She had gobbled up all the information she could on the beautiful flowers in her yard. Her favorites now included hyacinths, coneflowers, and Cock's Comb.

For some reason, the plot of the short story *Flowers for Algernon* suddenly in her head, Alys turned away from the resort grounds and turned her attention to the ocean instead. The rock covered beach made her think of the beach in Cape Elizabeth, Maine. She'd gone there with Iva. Not particularly ready to think too much about Iva or Maine or cancer, Alys focused her eyes on the path at her feet and wished she had a shot of bourbon for her run.

Chapter Three

AN HOUR LATER, THE T-SHIRT SHE'D THROWN ON over her bra soaked through with sweat, Alys stepped inside Pastriex to grab something on her way back to the suite. Fletch might be angry if he knew she had grabbed a specialty coffee after he made coffee for her this morning. But by now, he was probably settled in his own room or cottage, and he wouldn't have to know.

The bakery smelled heavenly. Alys flattened her hand over her stomach when it growled in protest at not being fed yet. At home, she might have had oatmeal or scrambled eggs by now, but she rarely splurged on baked goods. Not since Iva was gone.

She swept her gaze over the shelves laden with homemade jams and butters and cookies. Admired the gift packages of those items and more, all done up in cellophane and bows. Read the signs on the walls, her favorite being *All You Need is Love & Coffee*.

If only that were true.

The woman at the front of the line thanked the young barista and made her way to the door. Alys moved up in line, eyes on the chalked menu board behind the counter. She should just get black coffee. She probably hadn't had anything but black coffee since the last time she was here at this bakery.

The familiar voice now placing an order at the counter threw a steel knife in her throat. Claire. Afraid to move, as if Claire had eyes in the back of her head and would notice her, Alys held her breath. She turned her head slightly to consider a getaway, but there were already two people behind her in line. Any sort of commotion might draw Claire's attention.

When the barista stepped away to make Claire's drink, Alys slid her phone from her pocket and dipped her head over it to hide her face. She would have to face the woman soon enough, but she wasn't prepared now. A shower and makeup would help. She hadn't seen Claire face to face in several months, and she hadn't looked at her and felt like herself since the divorce.

Well. Before the divorce.

No texts to return, Alys scrolled through her social media feeds. She didn't keep up with anything anymore, so she had no idea what was going on in anyone's life. It made her look busy, though, so she made a point of reading Tamsin Baker's long political rant. Totally disconnected from her old friend and even more so from politics—who cared about the rest of the world when her own world had literally blown apart—she looked up as Claire stopped at her side.

"Allie."

Dread gushed up her throat and into her mouth, so she pressed her lips together and offered her oldest, dearest friend a cool nod. Because she couldn't meet her eyes, Alys stared at Claire's lips. Thin, pale, but Alys had always thought kissable, if she were a man. Claire didn't look a lot like Fletch, but there was a resemblance if you looked close enough.

Alys lifted her gaze for a moment, almost startled at the indifference in Claire's usually intense blue eyes. She wouldn't have known what to say anyway, but the cold emanating from her former sister-in-law snaked down her throat and wound through her lungs and left her unable to utter a word.

Claire looked the same. Perfectly messy blond beach waves. Blue eyes lined in soft brown. Eye shadow. Sun-kissed skin. Slender frame in the denim crop pants and simple white blouse. She held a cardboard drink carrier in her hands, and of course, Alys noticed the square cut diamond wedding ring on her finger. The only piece of jewelry Claire wore, it was gorgeous, and secretly, Alys and their other friends had tried it on a few days after Josh proposed to Claire. Never mind that Alys and Fletch were already married, and Alys wore her own platinum wedding band with a rock her friends were envious of.

The nail on her index finger was chipped, reminding Alys that in a few days Brooke and her mother and all her friends would descend on the resort. Alys would be expected to do the luncheons and the cocktails and manis and pedis with all of them. She would rather drink motor oil than be stuck in a crowd. Still, she was Ledger's mom, so she had to attend, like it or not.

"I'm sorry."

Claire's mumbled words drew her out of her thoughts. The line had moved forward; Alys stepped quickly to catch up. She had no idea what Claire was sorry for, but she didn't want to stand here and exchange pleasantries, especially when they were anything but pleasant, with her, and they sure as hell couldn't get into the nitty gritty life Alys now lived right here in front of the baristas and other innocent bystanders.

Alys tucked her phone back in her pocket and met Claire's eyes again.

"For your loss."

The words were quicksand, pulling her down, taking her under. Hours and hours standing in that goddamned line. The caskets side by side and Fletch there beside her. People touching her, shaking her hand and hugging her, and all she had wanted then was to crawl into the earth and cover herself in dirt.

I'm sorry.

So sorry for your loss.

You have our sympathy.

Fucking sympathy couldn't bring anyone back from the dead. The rational part of Alys knew her family and friends were sincere. That the other parents that paid their respects were sorry. People loved Jade and Kase, so many people would mourn them.

But mothers don't count. Mothers don't mourn. They die, too.

But Claire wasn't talking about Jade and Kase. They had been down that road a hundred fucking times, and it was one ugly ride that only got worse every time they traveled it.

"Iva."

Alys nodded and looked away. Claire hated Iva. Maybe in a general sort of way she was sorry Iva was gone, but then again, maybe when she found out—maybe Fletch had called to tell her—maybe she had thrown her fists in the air with a victory shout. It didn't matter; Alys didn't want to talk about Iva. Not to anyone. Certainly not to Claire.

Unsettled, wishing she could disappear, Alys glanced at the counter as the line moved again. The air seemed to move around her, the way it feels when a dog slips by and brushes your leg with its tail, and when she looked back, Claire was gone. A little sick to her stomach now—would Claire run to Fletch and tell him Alys had been rude?—her shoulders still slumped with relief. God, the next two weeks would be sheer hell. Why had she come early? Her thoughts of a few days of solitude were out the window, and she had nowhere to run.

ALYS SWALLOWED A MOUTHFUL OF CRANBERRY scone as she stepped into the suite. Her eyes took in the brass plaque on the door—The Valentine Suite, she and Fletch had wondered about the name before learning the room was named for a surname and not the holiday of love—but she forced herself to push the memories away.

It was easier when she still had Iva.

The door clicked closed behind her. Paper coffee cup tucked to her body with her arm, she broke off another bite of the scone and stopped at the couch when she heard Fletcher's voice. This couldn't be happening. He was supposed to be out finding another room while she was gone. Sure enough, though, a glance toward the oversized round dining table revealed his iPad, a folded paper—probably from three days ago, because he had a habit of buying a paper and taking a week or two to actually read it—and an empty water bottle.

Following Fletcher's voice, she found him on the balcony. The same balcony she had claimed last night for her bourbon. The scone stuck in her throat, she tried and failed to bark at him, anger boiling just under her skin.

Hearing whatever noise she ended up making, Fletch looked up at her and rolled his eyes. Phone pressed to his ear, he listened for a moment and tried to get a word in. Disgusted now, her appetite gone, Alys set the wax bag with the scone on the wooden railing and stared out at the choppy water. Surely, he hadn't waited around just to tell her goodbye.

"Hey."

He moved with stealth and was suddenly at her side. Alys watched him take her scone from the bag and take a bite.

"Eww." He frowned and put it back on the railing. "Why would you get cranberry? I like chocolate chip."

"I didn't bring it for you, did I?" She brushed her hands together and looked back over his shoulder into the living area. "Why are you still here?"

"No luck."

"What?"

"They're booked solid, Allie."

Alys hissed and tilted her head back to stretch. "Of course they are."

"Two weddings this week. And four conferences. I'm sorry."

She eyed him warily.

"I don't wanna sleep with you for the next two weeks."

"Interesting thing is you would fit on the couch." He said it off-handedly and added a quick shrug, like he was trying to play his words off as a joke.

"Even more interesting is that I booked first," she reminded him.

"Alys."

"Is this the only hotel or resort in Palos Verdes?" She folded her arms over her chest and tipped her head at him. Fletch stared back, apparently too stunned to speak. Regret pricked her all over when he finally nodded and stepped away from her.

"'Course not." He shrugged. "I'll find something else."

That wouldn't work. He needed to be here, too. For Ledger. Just as Alys had things she would have to do with Brooke and Claire and Brooke's mother, Fletch needed to be around for Ledger.

Well. Fletcher needed to be with his son as much as his son needed him.

"Fletch." She snatched the bag and crumbled it in her hand and hurried to follow him inside. She found him in the hall, bent over his suitcase. Her heart banged a bit when she saw the luggage tag. Why was he still carrying that around? Allie & Fletch Holland. Falls Church, Illinois.

"Christ, Alys, gimme a few minutes to pack up, okay?" He was pissed now. Alys snuck a quiet breath and squeezed her eyes closed.

"Just stay."

"I didn't even come close to the middle of the bed last night, in case you didn't notice." He crammed the clothes he had been wearing last night into the suitcase and zipped it closed. She bit her lip and eyed his toiletry bag visible on the bathroom counter from where she stood. "Not to mention that I've moved on, too. I'm not dying to jump you. Maybe that's a blow to your ego, but it's—"

"Stay."

"Just because Trish didn't come with me—"

"Dammit, Fletch, just stay." Alys moved at him, gave him a shove away from his suitcase before he could pick it up. "Just stay. You do your thing. I'll do mine. Whatever."

He hissed like air going out of a tire. Her belly twisted when he closed his eyes and pinched the bridge of his nose.

"Ledger asked me to come out early," he said quietly. Well, that sucked. She hadn't talked to Ledger in three or four weeks, and that last conversation consisted of him asking if she thought Brooke needed to invite distant relatives to the wedding. She'd said no, she hadn't seen her cousins in seven or eight years, and that had been that.

Of course, Ledge would want his father here with him.

Just the same as he wouldn't give a flying fuck if Alys was around.

"He's flying in Thursday. We're gonna golf."

She nodded when he looked at her, lest he think she was hurt. Or jealous. No way was she going to let Fletch know he'd scored a point. Eyes locked, they stood for a moment in silence. She waited for him to rail at her about Claire, but he didn't seem inclined to say anything.

"What're you drinking?" he finally asked.

She could lie. Tell him it was a latte or an americano or something. But he could just as easily call her bluff and ask for a drink.

"Just coffee."

Being divorced didn't take away how they could communicate without words, and she knew he was thinking about the coffee he made this morning. The mug she left sit when she rushed out earlier.

"Doug and Cindie Jeffries had a big anniversary party." He tucked his hands in his pockets. The motion drew her eyes to his hips, the gray shorts, and his hard, muscular legs. "Twenty-five years."

She nodded, because what the hell could she say to that? Tragedy pulled some people together and drove other people apart. The four of them were a perfect example.

"Iva used to tell me I had to let go of yesterday to move forward. We're not who we used to be, Fletch. We stopped fitting together."

He made a noise, sort of sounded like a sniffle, but his eyes were dry when she looked up. The look on his face, though, was hard to misread. Grief.

And not just for Jade and Kase.

"Iva." He nodded. "Was it bad?"

A startled laugh flew out of her mouth before she could catch it.

"Well, it wasn't good, Fletcher." She shook her head. "I need a shower."

He moved when she did, and they side-stepped each other, almost as if they were dancing.

"Do you...um..." He sighed and lifted a hand to rub the back of his neck.

"What?" She turned her back to him to grab clothing from her suitcase.

"Nothing."

She glanced at him, but he only shook his head.

"Never mind."

Chapter Four

THE SUNLIGHT OFF THE POOL WATER WAS A KNIFE IN her eyes. Alys shielded her eyes with her hand as she pushed the iron gate open with her other hand. It was quiet, but it was Monday, and she suspected even here at Kahalina Bluff, Mondays were slower. A young couple floated side by side on rafts at the other end of the pool. A few women sunned themselves on lounge chairs. Closer to her, Alys saw thick, muscular legs crossed at the ankle. She couldn't see the face, but she'd been married to him, and she'd slept beside him for twenty-five years, so she recognized Fletcher.

She had intended to go to the Sunshine Grill and grab a salad for lunch. Now that she'd accidentally seen Fletch, she felt obligated to say something to him. The music that played quietly from hidden speakers, so as not to foil the aesthetic, sounded a bit like Vegas club music. Interesting choice.

Fletch sat with his head tilted back, eyes closed. A paperback book lay on the pool deck, half under his chair. From where she stood, Alys saw that it was an old John Grisham novel. Fletch had read them all; Grisham was one of his auto buy authors. She wondered if he had found it out here by the pool and picked it up. That would explain the tattered cover.

"You gonna speak to me or just ogle the goods?" His lips barely moved when he spoke. Alys was startled, but she snorted with laughter and shrugged as she met his eyes. He did look good. Broad shoulders. Well-defined chest and biceps. He was tan already, too, she noticed when her eyes slid over his simple navy trunks. There was a pale line around his waistline where his trunks had rested at some point.

"Did you buy that tan before you got here?"

His smile was slow in coming. Uncomfortable standing over him when he was half-naked, Alys shoved her hands in the pockets of her white denim capris.

"Got it fair and square," he informed her.

"Yeah? When did you become a sunworshipper?"

His white teeth made her eyes hurt. She blinked and looked away. The rugged smile was dangerous. The sounds of conversations drifted over the pool deck from the Sunshine Grill. The smell of grilled chicken, maybe shrimp, lingered, and Alys' stomach growled again.

"Went to Cancun a few weeks ago."

The words were heavy like stones in her pockets. Cancun.

With Trish.

"Got it." She nodded. "I'm gonna—"

"Why do you do that?" He moved faster than a viper to swing his legs over the side of the chair and put his feet on the ground.

"Do what?" she asked as he gracefully climbed to his feet. She couldn't look him in the eye, but damned if she knew where to look. She struggled to keep her eyes off his chest. The shoulder she used to rest her head on at night when they went to bed.

"Run."

Irritated now, she sighed and shook her head. "I'm not running. I came down here to grab something to eat."

"Good." He nodded. "I'll go with you."

He watched her like he expected her to argue with him. So, she didn't.

"Good. You can buy."

He snagged his T-shirt, and Alys stole a glance at his waistline, at his trunks, when he tugged it over his head. Why hadn't Trish come with him for the wedding? Unless she was meeting him out here next week.

She waited while he grabbed his shades and wallet, and then he leaned over to pick up the paperback.

"What?" he asked when he looked at her again.

She shook her head and led the way to a high-top table on the edge of the patio. Fletch set his wallet and sunglasses down as she eased onto a stool.

"Beer me?"

She nodded and watched him walk the other way. In two years, they would both turn fifty. Forty felt like yesterday. The gray threaded through Fletch's hair had come with the accident. It hurt that tragedy had made him look better.

"What can I get for you to drink?"

Alys watched the waiter approach, catalogued his long blond hair held at the nape of his neck with an elastic, the diamond stud that twinkled in his ear, and the tattoo on his forearm. Looked like a dancing lion.

Would Jade think he was attractive?

An anchor pulled at her stomach, at her heart. Jade would never fall in love. There would be no mother-daughter shopping for a wedding dress. No wedding.

"Can I get a lager and a Mind Haze?"

"Of course," the kid answered with a nod. "Do you know what you want to order?"

"Um." She did. She wanted a salad. Fletch would eat a chicken sandwich. "No. My...he's in the restroom." She swallowed hard, the words ex and husband too big in her mouth, hard to shove them back down to her belly.

"Sure." The kid nodded. "My name's Xander."

Of course it is, she thought. But she only nodded and watched him head to the bar. Eyes on the tattoo on the back of his calf, she didn't realize Fletch was back until he dragged the chair back to sit down.

"Get me a chicken sandwich?" He slid his phone from the pocket of his trunks and put it on the table. Alys wondered if he had called Trish while he was gone.

"No." She shook her head. It was too familiar. Sitting with him like this, like they were still married. Reading each other's minds. It was enough that she knew he had walked away to use the restroom. That he would want a hazy IPA to drink.

He stared at her for a moment, almost like he wanted to challenge her. Thankfully, he finally shrugged and sat back.

"She didn't go with me," he announced after several moments of quiet.

"What?"

"Cancun."

Alys met his eyes.

"Trish didn't go with me."

"Oh." She wished Xander would hurry back with their beers. "So, you have someone new then?"

"No." He shook his head. "Trish and I aren't seeing each other anymore."

"You went to Cancun by yourself?"

"It was a long weekend. We had planned to go. Decided I would take the time off."

"And here you are, taking time off again."

She regretted it the second she spoke. This was different. This —Kahalina Bluff—was about Ledger and Brooke and nothing else. But the idea of Fletch spending a long weekend alone somewhere dug into her shoulder blades like claws.

It hurt.

"What happened?" she asked him.

"With Trish?"

Fletch had a way of looking at her that made her squirm. Intense and heavy, like she was the only woman in the world, and when they were married, Alys loved that about him. She hated it now.

"I'm sorry. I shouldn't ask."

He shrugged.

"She wants kids," he mumbled as Xander reappeared with their canned beers stacked in one hand and frosted pint glasses in the other. "Thanks."

"You bet." Xander's toothy smile directed at Fletcher made Alys wonder if he was gay. Or bi. Jade would be intrigued, for sure. If she were here, she would turn the moment into a soapbox, reminding Alys that experimenting with sexuality was good for personal growth.

If only Jade knew how Alys and Fletch lived now.

"Decide what you want?"

"She'll have a Caesar with grilled chicken and dressing on the side," Fletch spoke without consulting her. "I'll have the grilled chicken sandwich with fries."

"Comes with tomato and mayo. That okay?"

Fletcher nodded.

"What if I wanted the kale salad?" she asked because it rankled that he knew her so well.

"You hate kale." He shrugged.

Alys kept her eyes on the lager as she poured.

"Trish didn't want to be Ledger's stepmother?"

"She wanted babies." Fletch sounded disgusted. He popped the top on his beer and tipped the glass for his pour.

Alys covered her mouth with her hand, but the giggle slipped out.

"I forgot. What is she? Like twenty-five?"

"Thirty-six."

"Mmm." She took a drink and nodded.

"I didn't love her." He turned his head to look at the pool.

"I didn't ask."

They settled into silence. Fletch was still relaxed back in his chair, as if he didn't feel strung up and hanging over a barrel sitting here having lunch with her. Alys hated him a little bit for that. Being around him was hard.

She wasn't sure it would ever get easy.

"You get Iva's affairs straightened out?" He was still staring in the direction of the pool. Alys smooshed her lips together, wishing she could take the silence back. She didn't want to talk about Iva with Fletch. When she didn't answer, he looked at her expectantly. Alys arched her brows, realizing he wasn't going to let it go.

"Mostly." She nodded.

"What're you going to do now?"

She jerked her eyes up at his question.

"What do you mean?"

"With her house."

Iva was a trust fund baby, and she'd left her fortune to Alys. She didn't want to talk to Fletch about that, either.

"I'll probably stay," she mumbled.

"Really?"

She eyed him cautiously, wondering why he was surprised.

"For now." She shrugged. "Where would I go, Fletch?"

"You could sell it."

"And what? Find an apartment and pay rent?"

"They took her name off the door."

Alys nodded. "I know." The grief in her throat made the words small.

Fletcher sat forward suddenly and rested his elbow on the table. Alys watched suspiciously as he propped his chin in his hand and stared back at her.

"Do you remember building the treehouse for the kids?"

The memory made her flinch. Not the years of memories of the kids playing in the treehouse. But the summer she and Fletch built the house. Driving to the lumber yard with the windows in the truck down and Willie Nelson blaring from the cheap speakers. Fletch with the hammer in hand, holding nails between his teeth. Alys helping him hold the wood steady as he hammered away to build the framework. Taking a break and eating lunch meat sandwiches, legs dangling from the platform base, high up in the tree.

"Yeah." Her voice was thick still, with emotion. Too close, she dropped back in the chair and jerked her eyes away from his electric stare.

She didn't cry much. Not the night it happened. Not in the days that followed. There had been a few tears at the funeral, but not enough. Not enough for her family and friends to feel good about her level of grief. Not enough for her to feel any relief.

She cleared her throat now.

"Did you remember your tux?" She peeked back at him in time to catch his eye roll.

"Yes."

"Did you have a good time in Vegas?"

Ledger and his groomsmen had gone to Vegas for his bachelor party. Fletch had gone as part of the party, but also the man to foot the bill.

"It was alright," he mumbled. "Ledger was better behaved than any of his buddies."

"Well, Brooke has him by the balls," she reminded him.

"Brooke's a good girl."

"She can be a good girl and still have our son by the balls, Fletch." She took another drink.

"You think they'll have kids?" His voice was gruff. She wasn't surprised when he cut his glance back to the pool.

"I dunno." She licked her lips and sighed. "Probably not for a while. She likes her job."

"Do you want them to?"

"Not my business," she answered simply.

"Do you want grandbabies, Allie?" he snapped.

Alys blinked at him and shook her head. "No."

Chapter Five

FLETCH ASKED HER IF SHE WANTED TO GRAB DINNER together later. She didn't want to; she had come to Palos Verdes early for solitude. But she had to eat, and he knew it. She didn't particularly care what Fletch thought, but if things were at least courteous between them, Ledger's wedding might go smoother. She could at least give Ledge that much.

They walked side by side across the resort campus, but there was no conversation. Alys was lost in her own thoughts, thinking about the damned treehouse now, the day Ledger had hidden up there because he got in trouble at school, and he was afraid to face her.

Music blared from Howie's, and as they neared, Alys pulled up short. There was the roped off area where she and Fletch had stared at the ocean and drank their beers while they waited for a table. Fletch stopped walking several steps ahead of her and turned back. Their eyes met. It wasn't a bad cover band playing Foreigner songs, but the ghosts from that night flanked her anyway.

"We can just wait out here," he suggested. She nodded and watched him hurry up the two wooden steps to the hostess stand to put their name in. Alys folded her arms over her chest and hunched her shoulders in, not because she was cold, but because she needed to be small. And invisible, so the ghosts wouldn't realize she was here and come after her. Fletch was back at her side in minutes, but staring at him was no easier than reliving the memories.

"I shouldn't have come," she mumbled.

"To your son's wedding."

"Early," she added. A quick glance at his face broadcast his annoyance with her. "I shouldn't have come so early. I just..."

"Just what?" He stood with his back to Howie's, nearly toe to toe with her. Alys looked over her shoulder to judge how much room she had and backed a step away from him.

"I thought being out here would be...soothing."

Probably the wrong word, but she wasn't sure what word she was looking for. Other than solitude, and if she said that now, Fletch would get defensive and angry and tell her she didn't have to have dinner with him tonight.

"We have good memories here."

She gasped at his words and flinched when he tipped his chin down to give her another sharp, biting look.

"We don't?"

"Sure." She nodded and looked around a little desperately. "Kahalina Bluff's great. And then we lost everything."

"Not everything." He shrugged.

"Close enough."

"You say that shit in front of Ledge?"

She didn't, but that was because she rarely saw Ledger.

"How did you know Claire and Josh were here already?"

Fletcher watched the hostess escort another couple to a table and then looked back at Alys.

"She told me."

Alys nodded. "I saw her this morning. At Patriex."

"She told me."

"Nice."

"What's that mean?"

"Did she say that your bitch ex-wife didn't even say anything?"

Fletcher toed a renegade rock, loose from the landscaping, and shook his head. "She said you look like shit."

"Of course she did." Her laugh sounded bitter, but she was too exhausted to hide it and really, why bother? "I bumped into her after my run. We don't all walk around all dolled up twenty-four seven."

"That you've lost weight. That you look tired. Pale."

"Imagine that."

"She's not your enemy, Allie."

"Holland?" The hostess called. Alys breathed a tiny sigh of relief as Fletch ushered her ahead of him to follow the hostess to their table. She considered tucking a folded bill in the girl's hand for saving her from the conversation, but her money was zipped inside her little Kate Spade purse, and they sat down, and the girl was gone. And Alys was staring at Fletcher. Again.

"Hungry?" He picked up his menu.

"Not really."

"You got scallops last time, right?"

He was right, and it made her angry.

"Scallops and risotto."

She nodded when she realized he was staring at her over the top of his menu. He'd ordered lobster and shared bites with her. Alys looked away, let her eyes roam over a group of six at the table across from them. Memories of the warm butter dripping over her lip and Fletch leaning over close to kiss her. He pretended it was a quick peck, but he had licked her skin—his tongue like hot velvet on her face.

"Did they have a party?"

"What?"

"The Jeffries."

"Mmm." He put his menu down, making her regret the question. "No. They..."

"Fletch?" She tipped her head, her voice drawing him back.

"Um. I just saw it in the paper. Father Dawson said a special blessing over them at mass."

Alys chewed on her lip to keep her mouth from saying anything. Fletcher watched her pick up her menu.

"What?" He prodded when she ignored him and stared at the black text on the white background.

"I just can't believe you still go to church is all." She shrugged.

"Why would you say that?"

Zero to intensely defensive in a half a second. Alys sighed and looked at their approaching waitress with a huge swell of relief.

"Hi. I'm Mel, and I'll be taking care of you tonight." The woman was probably somewhere in her mid-thirties. Alys stole a glance at Fletch to see if he thought she was pretty. She was ballpark Trish's age. Maybe Fletch could score while he was here.

Then again, it wouldn't happen in her room.

"Can I get a shot of Knob Creek? Neat."

Mel nodded enthusiastically and turned to Fletcher who was now eyeing Alys instead of Mel.

"Glass of house chardonnay," he told her. Another nod, and then Mel launched into their specials, and Alys didn't hear a word, but she was glad for the reprieve. She was startled when Mel stopped talking and walked away.

"Are you getting lobster?" she asked him and then she hated herself for letting him know that he wasn't the only one who remembered the details from last time.

"No." He folded his hands over his closed menu. "I'm getting the blackened mahi-mahi special."

"I wasn't listening."

"No kidding." He pinned her in place with that intense stare. "What did you mean by that? What you said about church?"

"What do you think I meant, Fletcher?" She pressed her fingertips to her forehead as if she could magically make the memories disappear and push the headache away.

"What? Because I was sleeping with Trish? What about—"

"No," she spoke softly, because no one around them needed to hear this argument. "Jesus, that has nothing to do with it."

"Enlighten me."

"How can you believe in God? After what happened?"

He flinched. Her *man of steel* flinched and looked away, afraid to look her in the eyes. Fletch had begged her to lean, to let him love her through the loss, the grief. As if he was above hurting. She ran instead. She ran, and she kind of hated him, and then there was Trish.

And Iva.

"I don't know that I do, Allie."

His answer shocked her, left her speechless. When she didn't answer, he looked back at her, his eyes suspiciously bright.

"Why do you go then?"

He shrugged and shook his head. "Why do you drink?"

"Fuck you." She rolled her eyes. "You drink, too."

"Not like you do."

Probably not, but he had no right to call her out on that.

They were quiet for several long minutes. Conversations droned around them; Alys heard a woman nearby talking about someone named Betsy being seven centimeters dilated. A girl close by giggling and instructing her date to smile for real so they could selfie. Music—she recognized the song. "*You Make Me Feel Like Dancing.*" Again, Mel rescued her, this time with a lifeline. Alys eyed the amber liquid in her glass as she and Fletch placed their orders.

When they were alone again, Fletch sipped his wine, but Alys made a point of waiting even a minute or two after he set the glass down before sipping her whiskey.

"Do you miss her?" Her throat burned with her first swallow.

"Jade?" Fletcher's frown showed deep grooves in his forehead and the puffy skin under his eyes. "What the hell kind of question is that?"

"Trish," she corrected him. Because yes, they missed Jade, and no, she was not going to talk about their daughter here and now.

He sighed, all the fight draining out of him, and flopped backwards in his chair. Alys watched him closely for a moment, but when he shrugged his lips and locked his eyes on the horizon, she studied his chardonnay instead.

They didn't do house wines. The Hollands were wine snobs.

Well. The Hollands she used to know were wine snobs.

"I don't know."

"Really?" Intrigued by her ex-husband's relationship with another woman, by his seemingly blasé attitude about the breakup, she tipped her head and narrowed her eyes at him.

"I miss...having someone to talk to." He met her eyes. "Someone to come home to. I miss sex."

She snorted and rolled her eyes.

"When did you stop seeing her?"

"Couple months ago."

That surprised her.

"Did Ledger know?"

"Doubt it."

"Do you talk to him much?"

"Ledger?" Fletcher shook his head. "No. He calls once every few weeks. Maybe. Never has much to say."

"Do you?"

"Are you blaming me? For the relationship I have with our son?"

"No." She plucked her glass from the table again and sighed. "I'm worried about him."

"That's rich."

"So, I'm not throwing blame. But you are."

Fletcher arched his brows and delivered a dramatic shrug. "If the shoe fits."

"You're such an ass sometimes."

"Truth hurts, Allie-gator."

The nickname jolted her. She drank deeply and shook her head.

"Don't."

"Do you?"

"Do I what?"

"Miss Iva?"

Hardly the same thing, but she did. Ironically, she probably missed Iva more than he missed Trish.

"Yeah." She nodded, nostrils flared and eyes burning.

Funny. She could cry for Iva.

"I'm sorry." Fletcher looked uncomfortable now. "I shouldn't have asked."

Because they had only just ordered and the evening stretched much too far ahead of them to sustain this line of conversation, Alys took another fortifying drink—Ledger used to talk about his *forty-five vitamins* when he was seven—told herself to snap out of it, and asked Fletch about work. They used to share their workdays, back when they were married. After dinner. Dinner itself was conversation with the kids. What they learned at school. What they did for recess. What book they wanted to read next. Why Jade didn't steal second on the pass ball in the second inning. Alys and Fletch saved their talk until the kids were excused and doing homework or watching TV.

Recognizing the question for what it was, Fletcher grabbed it with both hands and spent the next half hour rattling about his sales quota and Madeline McGarrity's retirement and the fender bender the new intern had in a company car. Alys didn't give a damn about any of it, which made it so much easier to listen to. She even felt her mouth stretch a few times in a smile, and no, she wasn't one of those women who swore she would never smile again after what happened. She just didn't find a lot of occasions that called for it anymore.

They drank more with dinner. And they had another drink after dinner, and they bumped against each other on the walk back to the main residence of the resort. It felt almost chummy, and the liquor had warmed Alys, and she was so damned tired of holding herself, holding everything in check, and so it felt sort of good to let go a little.

At the main hotel, loud piano music pounded out of the bar, and Fletch nudged her with his elbow and nodded toward the bar in askance. She would be sorry tomorrow, she knew she would be. But going back to the suite now meant going to bed with her ex-husband where they would hug their sides and go back to being strangers.

The music was mostly jazzy, and Fletcher hated jazz. But he ordered her two fingers of bourbon and a beer for himself, and they cozied together at the bar and listened. The older woman seated at the grand piano had red hair obviously from a bottle and blue eye shadow that made Alys think of her first Cover Girl palette when she was thirteen. Her mother had helped her apply the makeup, but Alys hadn't been happy with her light hand.

"How do you even dance to this?" Fletch groaned. He wasn't asking her to dance. She knew that. He loved dancing; given too much alcohol, Fletcher Holland became a Travolta wanna be. But never to jazz.

"My grandparents did." She sipped and shrugged and then nodded at the couples gathering on the dance floor. "I like it."

"Since when?"

"Always. I just never listened to it because you didn't like it."

She watched over Fletcher's shoulder as more and more people crowded the tiny parquet floor.

"You ever think about getting married again?"

His question startled her. She turned to him and found him peeling the label from his bottle.

"No."

She didn't want love. She didn't want to love anyone. Ever again. And she damned sure didn't want anyone to love her again.

Drinks finished, they wound their way back through the crowd that had grown just since they had come inside. Fletch led the way, and without thinking, Alys linked her fingers through his so they wouldn't get separated.

Once in the lobby, she snatched her hand back. They walked to the suite in silence, the camaraderie of the night falling away. And after her nightly ritual with her facial cleanser and moisturizer—the very ones that touted special properties to prevent aging and obviously failed if Claire thought she looked tired and pale and gaunt—Alys changed into her pajamas and went to bed with a stranger.

Chapter Six

FLETCH WAS GONE WHEN SHE WOKE UP. ALYS LAY
still for a long time, listening first for him—maybe in the
shower or on the balcony working—and finally, once she
decided she was alone, listening to the whir of the fan over the
bed and the distant sounds of the ocean outside the open
French door. Vague memories of the night before crept into
her mind and brought with them a killer headache. She hadn't
been drunk last night, but she had certainly had enough that
this morning wouldn't be pleasant.

She had been doing that on a regular basis lately. Just another
thing that pissed her off—Fletch calling her on it, when all she
was doing was asking him about his faith.

Last night had been mostly pleasant, though. Then again, how
would she have dealt with spending the evening with him
completely sober?

The past year had brought more physical aches and pains, too.
She was getting older, sure, but she wasn't taking care of
herself anymore, either. Her shoulders and her neck hurt now

from sleeping on her left side all night, turned away from Fletch. She flopped over to lay on her back and rolled her shoulders, but it did no good.

Had they spoken to each other once they came back to the room? She didn't think so. Maybe a polite goodnight, though she doubted even that. Fletch had lingered outside on the balcony for a while, giving her plenty of time in the bathroom to get ready for bed. Wide awake, she had pretended to be asleep when he came to bed. Interesting that they had never reached this point in their marriage; they had to get divorced to find themselves in bed beside each other with nothing to say.

She needed a shower. The hot water and the steam would help the pain in her shoulders. From there, she would make coffee, because she didn't need to go to Patriex every day and pack on an extra five pounds when she went back home.

Work. She should check in, though she was on vacation. Still, as the head of PR at St. Lucy's, she should at least sit down and check her voicemail and email. Something she could do on the balcony while she sipped her coffee.

Rather than get up, though, Alys turned to her side and stared at the pillow still sunk in from where Fletch had laid his head. When they were married, if she didn't join him in the shower in the mornings—and she didn't often in the years when the kids were teenagers—she would take a moment before getting up and pull his pillow close and breathe in his scent. Take a minute to be thankful for her blessings; Fletch and the kids were always at the top of that list.

She reached for his pillow now but stopped with her hand in midair. Did he love Trish? Was he more upset about losing her than he had let on? Alys had no idea what she felt about it.

About Fletch with another woman. Part of her was relieved. Glad he was out or her hair. Happy that he had found someone else to make him happy, though she now knew better.

But part of her hated it, too. They had been together so long, the thought of him lying in bed with another woman, holding her, sleeping with his arm thrown over her waist, cut right through her middle and left her gutted. She had loved him fiercely.

When she left, Fletch had been surrounded by family and friends. Alys had been the one to strike out alone to shoulder her grief. Iva happened, so there was that, but it had been short lived, and now here, sleeping in the same damned bed with Fletch again, Alys felt more alone than ever.

The shower helped her sore muscles, and the coffee revived her brain and woke her up. She spent the better part of her morning on the balcony, though her mind wandered away from her email quite often, and her eyes wandered to the ocean more often than not.

She ate a protein bar for her lunch and decided she would sit poolside for a while. Fletch hadn't returned by the time she left, and she didn't want him to come back and find her still sitting in the suite as if she was waiting for him.

Her bikini days were over. Technically, they should have been over when she and Fletch were here to celebrate their anniversary. But they had been drunk on each other, drunk on life, and she had spent several days in a pretty skimpy bikini down by the pool. Fletch had talked her into it, reminded her no one at the resort knew them, and the kids would never have to know. There were no pictures of her in the black two-piece. There was no record of the way Fletch had stripped her of the bikini and mauled her on the balcony and in the dining room and in the hallway.

She felt self-conscious today, though, in the simple black one piece. There were people here who knew her now, and one of them had already commented on how bad she looked these days. Still, Alys chose a lounge chair at the far end of the pool —no deep end, the whole rectangular pool was no deeper than five and a half feet—and arranged herself comfortably. AirPods in, she chose to listen to jazz, and she let her mind wander to Fletch.

He had always hated jazz, so when they were married, they listened to rock and country. It was okay with her; she loved music, and she loved Fletch, and she loved his arms around her when they danced. She wondered now, eyes closed and chair reclined, if he danced with Trish much. He had been a little bit charming last night, unless it was the whiskey, which was possible.

Iva liked jazz, but Alys never listened to much music with her. Classical pieces now and then, but Iva had been addicted to podcasts, which tended to annoy Alys.

She lay with her eyes closed through several songs, and finally, she sat up with the intention of cooling off. Midday sun burned her skin, though, of course, she had slathered sunscreen on. Avoiding eye contact with anyone around her— four or five other chairs had been claimed since she had closed her eyes earlier—she put her AirPods in her bag and stood to jump in.

Ledger had a beautiful dive. It came to her now—the image of her oldest poised in a dive, body arced and hands pressed together leading the way into the water at the swim club back home. Her children were beautiful creatures by anyone's standards. Ledger was cut with hard muscle and olive skin and pretty blue eyes at fourteen. Brooke had a real catch for a fiancé. Unless, of course, Alys had fucked him up emotionally. After the accident.

Jade hated the diving board, but the girl swam like a fish.

Kase, her youngest—the biggest pain in the ass, class clown, and maybe the best-looking of all three—could dive like an Olympic athlete, but always chose, instead, to cannonball because it pissed off the most people at once.

She didn't jump in. With her heart so heavy now, she might sink straight to the bottom, and really, Alys wasn't sure she had the strength or the desire to surface again.

Instead, she lowered herself gingerly to sit on the side and dangle her feet in the cold water.

Overcome now with those memories, she squeezed her eyes closed and chanted—in her head—*let it go* over and over. In her head because she didn't want to be this kind of crazy. In public, her grief was stone cold and sharp like a Bowie knife. Being a cold-hearted bitch seemed easier and cleaner than coming unglued and burdening anyone else. *Let it go* because at least the babies she lost were at peace now, even if she never would be.

"You okay?"

She nodded in response to Claire's question, not even surprised to hear her ex-sister-in-law's voice. No question the next two weeks would be hell on her sanity, on the appearance of her sanity. Might as well just give into that now and go with the flow.

"Want something to drink?"

Alys blinked her eyes open and looked to her right. Blue toenails on tan feet. A gold ankle bracelet winked in the sunlight. Claire held her hand out toward her to offer her a pretty cocktail. Alys took it and mumbled thanks as Claire sat beside her, careful not to spill her own drink.

"Sex on the beach."

"I don't do that anymore." Alys sipped the cold drink. She would have to go easy since she'd only had a protein bar for lunch.

"Well, not on this beach." Claire's familiar throaty laugh made Alys' heart twinge a little. She sipped from her drink and set it down. Alys, still avoiding her eyes, watched her dip her hands in the water and splash her thighs and her belly. "Damn. That's cold."

Fletch had called her cold. When she filed for divorce. When she left. When she didn't cry.

"Fletch says you think I look like shit."

"You could use a cheeseburger," Claire answered simply.

Alys snorted and shook her head.

"I didn't mean anything, Allie."

She hadn't meant to be rude, and Alys knew it. But her concern rubbed like sandpaper on Alys' broken heart, so it didn't matter. She didn't want to hear it. She didn't want to sit here and play nice with Claire any more than she wanted to share the suite with Fletch.

"Where's Josh?"

Claire whipped her head around to stare at Alys, apparently surprised by her question.

"Golfing." She frowned. "With Fletch."

"Mmm." Alys nodded absently.

"Fletch didn't tell you?"

"We're not...really...talking, talking, Claire."

"You're sharing a suite."

"Out of necessity."

"Are you sleeping with him?"

Alys laughed and sighed. "Where's Hallie? Is she coming to the wedding?"

From the corner of her eye, Alys saw the way Claire tensed in response to the question.

"She gets in next Wednesday."

"She doing okay?" Alys asked, because she guessed from Claire's reaction that her niece was not doing okay.

But Claire only shrugged. Alys, eyebrows arched in surprise, nodded. She bit her lip to fight the bitter laugh, but Claire noticed.

"She's fine."

"Good." Alys hunched her shoulders. With her legs in the water, the sun felt good on her shoulders. She wondered what was going on with Hallie, but she had no right to ask. Not after the way she had shut Claire out of her life.

"Iva's?"

When Claire touched the simple silver band on her right ring finger, Alys flinched. She drew her hand away to rest in her lap, but when she felt Claire's eyes on her, she answered with a slight nod. It was sort of Iva's, but sort of hers. Not that she could explain that.

"Is it a wedding band?"

"No."

"Seriously, Allie." Claire leaned into her. The brush of her arm on Alys' felt too intimate. Alys shied away, desperate for space. Unfortunately, Claire noticed. "Fuck it. I give up."

"What're you doing?" Alys asked. But Claire jumped into the water. Alys watched her disappear and surface several moments later at the opposite end. Claire took a deep breath and dove back under. When she broke the surface near Alys' legs, she put her forearms on the side of the pool and lifted herself with ease.

"Hallie's flunking two classes," she announced as she hopped up to her feet. Cold water dripped from her to Alys's legs. "When we pressed her on it, she admitted to something happening at a campus party. So, she's in therapy now."

Alys swallowed hard.

"What happened?"

Claire squatted to grab her drink and look Alys in the eyes.

"I don't really wanna talk about it." She shrugged. "I guess I just wanted you to know you're not the only one hurting."

Alys gritted her teeth together. Claire was right.

"I get it. We all get it. We loved them, too. But I get it. They're your kids, and I can't begin to imagine the hole in your heart now. But you're selfish and ugly, and I'm done."

Selfish and ugly. Alys turned her head, unwilling to let Claire see she had hurt her.

"Selfish." She smacked her lips together with a nod. "Okay."

She had made a point to not break down, to not take advantage of Claire. Or Josh. Or Fletch. She had swallowed the heartache and put one foot in front of the other and marched herself through all of this without falling apart on them, and now Claire was calling her selfish.

"Yeah. Selfish." Claire nodded. She picked up her drink, eyes still hard and cold on Alys.

She had aged, too. Alys could see it now up close. Her face was bare, and there were fine lines around her eyes and her mouth. Maybe even though Alys had left, Claire had had to hold Fletch together.

Maybe *because* Alys left, Claire had had to hold her brother together.

"It's not a wedding band," she said quietly. "It was Iva's. It's engraved. The words *My Heart*. Her grandmother gave it to her. Iva gave it to me when...before..."

"And that's how you filled your heart?" Claire tipped her head. Uncomfortable under Claire's heavy stare, Alys lowered her eyes and watched beads of water slide over her ex-sister-in-law's golden-brown skin. "With someone else?"

"Why do you have to say that? Why do you have to make it about that?"

"Wasn't it?"

Alys let her eyes climb back up to meet Claire's when she shrugged and tipped her head. She worked her mouth to answer Claire, but she didn't know what to say.

"Can I sit? Or are you gonna keep blowin' me off?"

Alys dipped her chin to her chest, desperate to take a deep breath, but unable to with the knife in her windpipe. She told Claire to sit, but it hurt to speak, and she wasn't sure the word actually came out of her mouth, until finally, Claire eased back down to her butt and put her legs in the pool again.

"Is Hallie okay?"

Their eyes met, so Alys saw Claire's tears well up.

"Some guy drugged her drink." She sniffled. "She's still not sure what happened, but she woke up in someone's bed."

"No one saw anything?"

"Her girlfriend says they were at the party together. But they got separated. She ended up on the patio with a bunch of guys, but apparently, she's okay."

"I'm sorry."

Alys' whisper hung in the air for a few minutes.

"She drinks so much now," Claire continued. "Losing Jade..."

Alys nodded when Claire glanced at her. The girls had been attached at the hip.

"I'm not." Alys took a deep breath and started again. "I'm not being selfish."

"Right." Claire nodded. "You left my brother. At the hardest time in your lives, you walked out. And almost immediately, you found someone else. That's pretty fucking selfish if you ask me, Allie."

"I couldn't handle my own emotions." Alys pressed her lips together and surveyed the pool deck. People came and went constantly now, old and young, women and men. Was everyone here carrying ugly baggage like she was? Like Claire was now? Or were some people untouched by life's brutality? "How the hell was I gonna handle his?"

"You're supposed to do it together."

Alys shook her head. "I didn't want to tear him down with me."

"Bullshit."

"I don't think..." Alys cleared her throat. "I just can't do it, Claire. Not anymore."

"And what about Iva?"

Iva happened, but Alys had never been able to explain it to anyone. She didn't understand it herself.

"I mean, were you in love with her?"

Alys bit her lip. She had no answer for Claire. Because even now, she had no idea what Iva had been to her.

"Um." She sighed. "I need food."

"This is what I mean," Claire said softly.

"I'm selfish because I want food."

"Because you're running away. Let me in, Allie. Let me listen. Give me that gift."

"Believe me, my thoughts....my feelings right now are anything but a gift, Claire. They're a nightmare, and I need to eat something, because I was hungover this morning, and I've only had a protein bar to eat today."

"Your trust would be a gift."

Alys dabbed at her eye. She wasn't about to cry out here at the pool.

"It was never that I don't trust you—"

"Of course it is." Claire rolled her eyes. "You're on a little whoa-is-me island, being a martyr with your grief, and you don't trust anyone to get it. To coddle you. To save you."

"Maybe I don't wanna be saved."

"Doesn't your son deserve better than this?"

"Sure, but what's better for him? Half of me? Or nothing?"

"Why Iva?"

Alys stuck her hand in the air and waved when she noticed a waiter making his way around the pool. He nodded to let her know he saw her.

"I don't know." Before Claire could argue, Alys added, "I don't, Claire."

Chapter Seven

THE TWINS WEREN'T IDENTICAL, AND OFTENTIMES, Alys thought Jade was more like Kase than Ledger. No wonder Jade and Kase were close, despite their difference in age.

She still didn't know why Jade was with Kase that night.

She did her damndest to not think about it, although the Jeffries had hammered at her and Fletch in the first few months, finally threatening them with legal action when coaxing and begging for explanations didn't work. Alys wasn't sure how Doug and Cindie thought they would know what the hell had happened. The cops had recreated the scene based on the skid marks on the road and the tire tracks off-road.

And the way the front of the car was wrapped around the tree.

But *no one* knew why. Alys and Fletch didn't know why. What led to Kase getting in the driver's seat after drinking. They hadn't handed the liquor to their sixteen-year-old. That being said, Alys would have given Doug and Cindie everything, their entire world, but she knew for a fact it wouldn't do anything for them. Nothing would bring Zoey back, and Alys knew it because nothing would bring Jade or Kase back.

Going through Jade's things after everything happened, after the funerals, had been one of the hardest things Alys had ever done. Kase's too, but Alys had been mostly alone with Jade's things. Fletch had taken one look at Jade's oversized teddy bear on her bed and walked out of her apartment without a word.

Alys wanted to run, too. To follow Fletch out of the two-bedroom apartment their daughter had rented. She didn't, though. Not because she was brave or tough, but because she couldn't bear the thought of getting back in the car with Fletch and driving home in the silence that stood between them since the night of the accident.

She moseyed through her daughter's apartment, feeling like a voyeur and wanting desperately just to know Jade in every way possible, especially in ways she hadn't been allowed to know her. They had been close, but every girl keeps secrets from her mom, and each secret Alys found that used to belong to Jade chipped another little piece of her away.

The earrings on her bedside table had brought tears to her eyes. They were Alys', and when Jade was in junior high, she snuck them out of the jewelry box on Alys' dresser to wear to a dance. Alys had scolded her, because thirteen-year-old girls didn't need diamonds. But she'd given them to Jade on her sixteenth birthday, along with a diamond necklace.

Jade had never worn the earrings, though she wore the necklace all the time. Finding the diamond studs on the nightstand gave Alys a stomachache.

She found a stash of old birthday cards in the kitchen, in the drawer next to the silverware. Some of them were signed by Alys' mom, which had been touching in a completely different way. A pack of cigarettes with four missing in her desk drawer. That shocked her.

The love letter from someone with the initial R left her empty. Whoever R was—and Jade never mentioned anyone, not even in passing—had spent some incredible time with her daughter and was very much in love with her and hurt that Jade didn't feel the same.

If her brain hadn't shorted the night they found out about the accident, she might have asked Ledger about the things she found at Jade's. Surely, he would know. She didn't ask him, though. Ledger retreated into himself, and Alys let him, because it was easier for her.

She supposed maybe that did make her selfish.

She would do the same if she had to relive the nightmare.

Dinner tonight was at Fury, but this time, it wasn't just her and Fletch. Claire and Josh joined them at the upscale beach front bar and grill. Alys had thrown up twice while she was trying to get ready. Fletch had tapped on the bathroom door and then barged in to check on her, accusing her of getting drunk at the pool.

Maybe it was a combination of the drinks and nachos she had shared with Claire. Maybe it was the sun. Maybe it was nerves. Alys had felt a rush of panic earlier when she walked into the suite to find Fletch leaning over the table in the dining area, eyes on his computer screen. Still dressed for the golf outing, he had glanced at her—she noticed the way his eyes moved over her shoulders and breasts before sliding back up to meet hers—and announced that they were having dinner with Josh and Claire.

Now, as the sun set over the ocean, Alys felt another panic attack coming on. They used to hang out with Claire and Josh all the time. These three people knew her better than anyone else in the world, and it was exhausting when she couldn't hide.

More drinks, thank Christ, or she might not have made it this far into the vacation, let alone through Ledger's wedding weekend.

"So, I heard Trish is already seeing someone," Josh announced. Alys knew from the way he flinched that Claire had smacked his leg or kicked him. Alys peeked at Fletch to see his reaction, curious when he answered with a half-hearted shrug.

"What?" Josh snapped at Claire. "For God's sake, Claire. Alys knows Fletch was seeing her, and Alys is the one who filed for divorce, anyway."

"Trish wants a family," Fletch told Josh.

Alys dragged her eyes over Josh's round face and down to her wine. She was trying to be social tonight. Normal. Not shooting-whiskey-to-get-drunk-selfish. She had filed for divorce, and she knew when Fletch asked Trish out, because he texted her to tell her. She hadn't responded. She hadn't cared.

Now she wondered if they had sex on their first date.

"Oh boy." Josh grimaced. "Nobody our age wants to do that again."

"Truer words," Claire mumbled. Alys flicked her gaze up to study Claire for a moment. She wondered about Hallie. Had her niece been raped? She could have asked Claire if she had reported it. If there had been a pelvic exam. But that was a little bit like Claire asking her what Kase's blood alcohol level was after the accident. They all knew Kase was drunk. No one needed a detail so exact.

Except maybe Doug and Cindie Jeffries.

"So, what's next?" Josh asked Fletcher, and Alys wondered what the hell they had talked about on the golf course that made them put this conversation off until now.

"I dunno." Fletch shook his head.

"That blonde at the bank is into you," Claire told him.

What blonde at the bank? Alys didn't remember any blondes at their bank.

"I think I'm just gonna lay low for a while," Fletch said quietly.

"Yeah?" Josh needled him and wagged his eyebrows. He wasn't being cruel; Alys knew him well enough to know that. They used to share everything and tease and talk and laugh about everything they shared. "No more sex in the trunk of the car, huh?"

Alys, glass at her lips, nearly choked on a swallow of cab.

"The trunk of a car?" She looked at Fletch, a little stunned and a lot confused. "How and why?"

"You don't wanna know." He shook his head. Alys glanced at Josh and Claire. Obviously, Josh knew, but did Claire? Was Alys the odd man out?

"I do, though," she insisted, pulling on a mask of indifference. Pretending to be amused rather than jealous.

"It was after a barbeque," Fletch told her with a frown. "At her friend's house. We were both a little drunk, and she was kind of handsy. We had sex in the hatch of her CR-V. It wasn't a trunk."

She and Fletch used to be that way. Couldn't keep their hands off each other. Jealousy rushed through her veins like flame on gasoline. She nodded and sipped her wine rather than saying anything. From the corner of her eye, she saw Claire open her mouth to speak. If she said a word about Iva, Alys might throw her wine in her lap.

"Told you." Fletch fussed with his silverware setting. They were at a high-top table, thank God, because Alys couldn't imagine being stuffed into a booth with him.

"No." She swallowed and shook her head. Even managed to pull up what she hoped was a blasé smile. "Just thinking you were both drunk and leaving a party." She licked her lips and met his eyes for moment. "Seems kind of...irresponsible. After what happened."

"We didn't leave, though," he argued quietly. "Not for a few hours."

"Hmm." She nodded. "Hours. You've upped your game."

The insult did its job, but Alys didn't feel any satisfaction when Fletch snapped his mouth closed and stared at her with a stone face.

"Mmm." Claire tipped her head. "Didn't you tell me about a night out here that went on for hours?"

"You told my sister?" Fletch cringed.

Alys turned her head to Claire, wondering if she should be angry with her for taking the sting out of her insult or relieved that she had thrown the comment out and killed the tension. Claire studiously avoided her eyes, though, so she turned her attention to the menu.

"I feel like all we do is eat on vacation," she mumbled, more to herself than as conversation. "Why is that?"

"Because we do," Josh answered. "Remember that steakhouse we stopped at in Texas?"

"Ohmygod, that was like seventeen years ago," Claire groaned. "God, you two ate so much I thought you would break the weight things on the car."

"Axels, babe." Josh shot her a frown.

"Whatever." Claire sighed. She closed her menu and sat back in her chair.

"What're you gonna have?" Fletch asked her.

"Calamari."

"That's an appetizer."

"Well, I'm having it as my meal."

"What about you, Allie?"

She hated that they had all sunk back into calling her Allie. She hadn't been Allie since the kids were killed. Iva had only called her Alys.

"I might get scampi."

It felt wrong to sit here with her ex and his family and carry on like their lives hadn't exploded. Alys was uncomfortable sipping wine and teasing with Claire and Josh about dinner items. But what else could she do? If she called it a night and walked back to the suite, there would be a strain on their exchanges, and Ledger and Brooke would notice.

Dinner was more of the same conversations. Memories with and without the kids. Talk of work. Murmurs about Hallie, worry that she wouldn't get past what had happened. Or more to the point, never knowing for sure what happened. Talk about Ledger and Brooke, about Brooke's position at the hospital and Ledger's engineering career. Rumblings about whether or not they would have kids. Alys pushed the image of a tiny Ledger swaddled in a newborn baby blue blanket out of her head and chased it with a gulp of wine. Practical discussion about the wedding day.

When dinner was over, the four of them wandered around campus for a bit to walk off the calories. Alys wasn't as stuffed as the others claimed to be, but again, thoughts of returning to the suite and returning to the strangers they had become made her panicky, like her skin was on too tight. Thoughts of being alone in the silence with Fletch gripped her lungs and squeezed, and she couldn't breathe.

They stopped at the outdoor bar called Currents. This one had been under construction when she and Fletch were here last, so there were no ghosts lingering to haunt her. She and Claire claimed a table on the patio while the guys ordered drinks. A jukebox pounded out vintage Springsteen, and a light breeze claimed a pile of napkins at a nearby table.

"Gonna shoot pool," Fletch announced when he put a shot of bourbon down by Alys' elbow. She nodded, irritated that he could still read her so well. She didn't want wine, but she would have preferred he got her wine so he could be wrong.

"How can you drink that crap?" Claire watched her sip. "It's so hot."

"I like the way it burns," she mumbled.

"I'm sorry." Claire turned her head to watch Fletch and Josh take up pool cues across the deck.

"For what?"

"What Josh brought up at dinner."

"He dated her for a long time," Alys said simply. "I'd have to be stupid to think he wasn't fucking her."

"Still." Claire shrugged.

Because it did hurt just a little, Alys nodded and mouthed the word *still* as she sipped her whiskey. Claire watched her set the tumbler down and then she reached over the table and touched the ring on her hand again.

"Tell me."

"Counseling." She shrugged.

"Iva was your counselor? Isn't that unethical?"

The wine with dinner and now the bourbon wiggled its fingers in her brain. She didn't talk about Iva, but that was the thing. After she left Fletch, she only talked to Iva, and now Iva was gone.

"She was in the building where Fletch and I were going."

"Marriage counseling?" Claire asked softly.

"No." Alys rubbed her eyes. "I loved him, Claire. You know we were happy."

Claire arched her eyebrows as if to argue, but to her credit, she didn't comment.

"After...the kids were...after the accident. We did a few sessions. A few together. A few by ourselves. I met Iva one night when I left my appointment."

Claire nodded, but she looked upset or confused.

"But why?" She tucked a chunk of hair behind her ear. Alys held her breath. "I'm not trying to be argumentative. I'm not being hateful. I'm just...I don't understand, Allie."

"I didn't leave Fletch for Iva."

"But you left Fletch. And ended up with Iva."

Alys shrugged. "Not really."

Claire ducked her head for a second. When she lifted her hand to wipe at her eyes, Alys was startled to realize she was crying.

"We all lost Jade and Kase, and I know I can't hijack your grief. I get it, Alys." Claire nodded. "And I get that marriage is—I get that what happened with you and Fletch is between you two. I don't know what went on, what was said. But you left me, too. I lost you, too, and I don't..." She met Alys' eyes and shrugged. "I still don't know why. Or what happened."

"I couldn't breathe," Alys whispered. "With the guilt. The grief. The memories and the questions." She glanced at the guys and continued when she saw they were still at the pool table. "With his grief on top of mine. With Ledger on top of that. I couldn't fucking get a breath, and I literally ran into Iva one night, and she took my hand and told me to stop. We were in the waiting room at the clinic, and she held my hands and looked in my eyes and told me to breathe."

"And?" Claire leaned over the table, anxiously awaiting the rest of the explanation. "You fell in love with her?"

"No. We just...we became friends."

"So, she wasn't your new Fletcher. She was your new me."

"No, Claire." Alys groaned. "No. We just—we started meeting for coffee. We talked. She was someone who didn't know me. Or Fletch or the kids. She didn't know about all the baggage, so it wasn't something I had to unpack and dig through when we were together."

"And I made you do that?" Claire touched her chest. "I made you wallow in it?"

"I know that you meant well. You wanted to help. Maybe with someone else, you would have been perfect. But I needed to breathe, and I couldn't do that around you guys."

"But how did you go from meeting for coffee to moving in with her?"

"I needed a place to go when I left Fletch. She had a huge house to herself."

"Were you sleeping with her?"

"No." Alys shook her head. "No. Not like that."

"I don't know what that means." Claire wiped at her eyes again and pushed her hair off her face. "Fletch said he saw you two once. That you kissed her. He saw you in a kiss with tongues, and so you can lie to me all you want, but he saw you."

"That doesn't mean I was sleeping with her."

"You loved her."

"I did, yes. But no, I wasn't in love with her."

Claire drew in a deep breath and picked up her drink. "'kay. I'm gonna—"

"Iva was bisexual, yes. And yes, she said she had feelings for me. But we weren't sleeping together. There was a kiss or two, but she knew I wasn't comfortable with it. And she knew—"

"She knew what?" Claire dared her.

Alys shook her head. Iva had insisted it wasn't simply that Alys was uncomfortable about being with a woman, but that she was still in love with Fletcher.

Chapter Eight

It was nearly midnight when Fletch unlocked the door to the Valentine Suite and ushered her inside. Six hours for dinner and drinks and true confessions. *After* spending the day at the pool with Claire. Alys was exhausted, but too keyed up to sleep. Still, being back here alone with Fletch was painful, like the world stopped as the door clicked closed behind them.

She avoided his eyes as he made his way to the balcony and she to the bathroom to get ready for bed. They had too many nights left of doing this. The silence between them was huge and powerful, and as she brushed her teeth, she wondered about getting a room somewhere else. Being off the resort campus would get her out of the dinners and dates with Claire and Josh, too.

But the thought of being somewhere else alone while they were here, together, was a knife in her belly.

Instead of going to bed when Fletch took his turn in the bathroom, Alys sat on the lounge chair on the balcony. She couldn't make out the horizon in the darkness; the black of the ocean rolled off into the black of the sky somewhere. Knowing that would never change was comforting.

"What're you doing?"

She shook her head when Fletch spoke behind her.

"I'm so tired," she whispered. "But I don't know if I can sleep."

"What's wrong?"

She shot him a look of disbelief over her shoulder.

"You and Claire looked deep in conversation earlier."

She nodded.

"Not gonna tell me?"

"She asked me about Iva."

Fletch propped himself against the door and folded his arms over his chest. The gray T-shirt he wore pulled taut over his shoulders. Alys eyed the muscles in his arms and then reminded herself that he liked younger women now.

"And you told her things?"

"What things do you think I told her?"

His whole body moved when he took a deep breath. Alys felt a pang of regret when he lifted his hand and squeezed the back of his neck.

"I probably don't want to know."

Finding out about Fletch and Trish having sex in the hatch of her SUV hadn't been the highlight of her evening, either.

"Goodnight." He pushed off the door and turned his back to her. Alys mumbled goodnight, but she didn't move. Not for several long quiet moments. She wasn't thinking about Jade and Kase tonight. Not at the moment.

But Iva. The pain in her gray eyes when she had confessed to being in love with Alys. Her bravery when she told Alys she didn't need her to love her back.

No idea how much time had passed, Alys stepped inside and closed the door. She padded bare foot to the kitchen for a drink of water. Bottle in hand, she rested her elbows on the counter and stared at the other bottle, the one she had begun to rely heavily on to get through even the easiest of days.

"Allie?"

"What, Fletch?" she asked with a sigh.

"Don't drink more. Please?"

"I'm not." She straightened and waved her water bottle at him.

"It's after one. Come to bed."

The words used to mean so much more. Now it simply meant that Fletch was worried that she would break open the bottle of whiskey the second he turned his back on her. She wanted to argue but only capped the water bottle and put it back in the refrigerator.

He hadn't moved when she turned to the door. Lamplight glowed faintly from the living room, giving Alys a good look at his strong, muscular legs beneath his shorts. Deeper in the kitchen, she was in darkness and free to drink him in.

"I need—"

"Aren't you—"

They spoke at the same time. A small smile perked his lips up, and he nodded at her. "You first."

She was going to say *I need this to end*. Because she couldn't get used to sleeping with him again. And then get used to sleeping alone again. She wouldn't do that to herself.

"Never mind." She shook her head.

She knew when he stepped closer that he was going to kiss her. She knew she would kiss him back. What she didn't know was how good he would taste and how much it would hurt. He had kissed her forehead the day she walked out. Papers filed. Marriage ended. Love supposedly gone. A chaste kiss on her forehead. Before that, there had been a frenzy of hard, animal sex as they both tried to drive the demons from their minds. Kissing then had been teeth crashing and biting, and both of them cussing and crying out.

Now, though. This kiss was cautious and tender.

Not sweet. God, no. They had been through far too much to share a sweet kiss on a night like tonight after the loss they had shared. His fingers hovered near her chin, just short of touching her. His lips brushed hers, lazy and light. Back and forth. Again. And again.

The fingers of his other hand were soft on the back of her neck, under her hair. That touch was almost more intimate than the kiss. Until she gasped at the shock of how badly she wanted this. And more. And then he stroked her lips with his tongue, and she responded, and the kiss was slow and sad and so intimate, it hurt.

Tears in her eyes, she broke the kiss and backed away from him.

"Allie."

She shook her head and held a hand up to stop him. No excuses. No apologies. She didn't want to hear his voice right now. Because it was laced with pain, and she couldn't handle his pain on top of her longing for him.

Fletch bit off a curse as she slipped by him and made her way to the bedroom on trembling knees. She considered locking herself in the bathroom, but why? She had kissed him back; she couldn't deny that. It was a mistake, fueled by desperation and alcohol. Not a big deal. Instead, she crawled into bed and turned her back to his side. She stared into the darkness when he eventually joined her, though she could tell he was lying on his back.

"Were you in love with her?" she asked.

"No." He sighed. "I liked her. But no."

"Is that why you didn't want to have kids with her?"

"Alys, I had my children. I don't want to do that all over again."

"But you could still be with her."

"What do you think Ledge would have said if I would have married her? Gotten her pregnant?"

"Remember the night he scored twenty-seven points against Havana?"

"Could I forget?" Fletch laughed softly. "How about the night Kase threw a no-hitter?"

"Mmm." Alys did remember that night, too. She remembered the big things. The little things, like Kase giving her the evil eye when she put him in time out. The way Jade held her mouth when she was trying to memorize something for school. The way Kase would wrinkle his nose before he sneezed. It was all the other everyday things that she would never remember that bothered her.

"Allie?"

"What?"

"Do you hate me?"

The edge in his voice stole her breath. She squeezed her eyes closed and shook her head.

"No. I don't hate you, Fletch." She didn't hate him. She didn't wish him away; she just couldn't let herself love him again.

***

ALYS WASN'T SURE SHE HAD SLEPT AN HOUR through the night. That damned kiss made sleeping beside Fletcher harder, and every time he shifted or turned over, she flinched, afraid her body would betray her and curl up to him. The drapes barely moved with the breeze, and the heat coming off her ex-husband's body was enveloping, and she constantly kicked the sheets off only to wake a few minutes later with her sweat-slicked skin chilled.

She dragged herself from bed before six, dressed quietly for a hike, and slipped out of the suite unnoticed. They hadn't discussed plans for the day, so she had no idea what Fletch was doing. But she needed a break. A breather. Ledger and Brooke would arrive over the weekend. Alys needed to be alone to find the strength to get through the next week.

It felt good to slide behind the wheel of the rental. She cracked the windows, opened the sunroof, and reveled in the morning chill. Chris Stapleton's bluesy voice kept her company as she drove aimlessly.

They found Kase's Charger bent up like an accordion around the huge Oak tree on the corner of Front and Ballard Streets. A few more blocks and he might have ended up in the river. As unbearable as the loss was, Alys couldn't imagine never knowing where her kids were or what had happened to them. Then again, the car would most likely have been found eventually. Still, the thought of their bodies in the car submerged in the river made her sick.

She dreamt about that once.

Zoey was in the backseat. Which made zero sense to Alys. Then again, she couldn't begin to imagine why Jade was with them at all. When that night had started, Kase and Zoey left the house together, holding hands, laughing at something Fletch had said to them.

Alys narrowed her eyes in thought, trying to recall what he'd said.

Something about a dance off. Fletch had declared he was a much better dancer than Kase. He'd demonstrated a few ridiculous moves, and Kase had dragged Zoey out of the kitchen, telling Fletch not to hurt himself.

Alys could still hear his voice as he climbed into this car. Zoey had said goodbye to her. They had long since gotten past the Mrs. Holland thing, but Zoey had never called her Allie. At the car, Kase had stopped, hand on the top of the door, and looked at Alys, who stood in the garage watching them go.

Almost like she had known something big was coming. Something bad.

"Love you, Mom."

His last words to her. He said them to her every night when she went to bed, because he was always up later than she was.

She'd waved at him that night and called goodbye, but now she hated herself for not saying she loved him, too. She told him so every night when she went to bed. She hadn't that night, because she didn't want Zoey to think he was a mama's boy.

As if Zoey hadn't been around the family enough to know he wasn't. That they were just close-knit. Easy with their emotions.

Except they weren't anymore.

She couldn't remember the last thing Jade said to her, and that bothered her, too. They had talked about Jade's job—that she was working a new account. As a young, brand new professional, Jade had been a bundle of nerves and excitement. Alys felt a lick of sadness now, remembering that she had looked at Jade sometimes and felt a flash of envy of her daughter for having the world at her fingertips.

Now Jade rested in St. Mark's Cemetery, and Alys battled another round of nausea. Who the hell felt envious of her own child? Maybe she had brought this on. Maybe she was at fault.

Jade had been thrown from the car. Another thing that bothered Alys, because Jade was a rule follower, and she would have been wearing her seatbelt. Then again, unspoken rules in their house made smoking bad, and Alys had found the cigarettes in Jade's apartment, so maybe she didn't know her daughter nearly as well as she thought she did.

Kase had died en route to the ER. Steering column had crushed his lungs. Internal bleeding. Alys had stopped hearing the doctor at that point. Didn't matter. Jade made it to the ER, but she had bled out in the exam room. Her kids were gone. Life as she knew it would never be the same with Jade and Kase gone.

Zoey, in the backseat, still sustained fatal injuries. Just took her a little longer to let go. Alys had gone around the bend a few times about that. She'd felt so awful for Doug and Cindie, having to watch a machine pump air into their daughter's lifeless body. Wondering if she would ever wake up. If she would recover once she did wake up. The endless days of hospital rooms and the beeping of the monitors and the coming and going of strangers in your life—shifts changing just as you get comfortable with someone new, and then all of it lasting so long, you learned everyone on all the shifts. And finally, you had to let go anyway, and you had an audience of people watching you break down.

On the other hand, Doug and Cindie had days with Zoey that Alys didn't get with her kids. They were given precious moments to sit with Zoey and hold her hand and talk to her. Cindie Jeffreys had been given time to stare at her daughter and memorize every freckle and every scar and every eyelash. Time to stroke her skin, to press her own fingers over Zoey's arms and face.

Time to say goodbye.

Alys parked the rental car in the small rectangular parking area of the park she and Fletch had found the last time they were here. She didn't remember the name of it, and she hadn't been paying attention when she pulled in just now. She hadn't been paying attention for most of the drive on the Pacific Coast Highway, if she were being honest. Too consumed by thoughts of the kids.

She wasn't dressed for a serious hike, but the fresh air that filled her lungs on the first deep breath almost seemed easier to breathe. The sun remained partially hidden behind clouds and morning fog, but Alys saw it in the hint of shadows around her. Rather than wander off on her own on a trail, she popped the hatch on the back of her SUV and climbed in. Facing backwards, legs dangling, she focused on the view of the ocean and not the visual of Fletch and Trish having drunk sex in the back of her SUV at her friend's party.

Some days she envied the Jeffries the goodbye time they had. But really, sitting and watching your child breathe—watching a machine pump oxygen into your child's lungs and fearing that removing that machine would be the end. Was that any easier than the sudden way she and Fletch lost Jade and Kase?

Nope. Because watching your children die, burying your children wasn't the natural order of things, and it wasn't supposed to be this way. Ever. Didn't matter the circumstances, the whys, the hows—she and Fletch, Cindie and Doug, they'd all lost someone they loved more than life, and nothing was going to fill the void that loss had created.

Chapter Nine

SEEING HER SON SHOULDN'T HURT, BUT JUST A glimpse of him from across the room stole her breath away. Tall, broad-shouldered like Fletch, he was an imposing figure. He didn't wear a permanent scowl, but his face appeared cut from stone, making Alys wonder if people were afraid to approach him. Was he close to anyone other than Brooke?

He used to smile a lot, though he had never been the cutup that Kase was. Ledger had a dry humor, and it was easy to miss it if you weren't paying attention. Alys had no idea how he was doing after losing his twin and his little brother. She spoke with him as little as she possibly could, telling herself the distance was for his sake. Ledger didn't need a ghost for a mother. Her walking out on his father, on Ledger's life, had to be easier for him than a mother who couldn't love him anymore.

He wore golf clothes, though she doubted he would golf today. According to Fletch, their flight had landed late morning, and he and Brooke had just arrived not even an hour ago. Alys assumed they would spend the rest of the day together and tomorrow spend time apart—Ledger with Fletch and Brooke with her family.

Ledge had grown out of hugs and love yous when he was still in grade school. Back in those days, when Alys tucked him in or just told him goodnight from his doorway as he got older, he would simply nod and grumble something incoherent when she said she loved him. Hopefully, he was good about telling Brooke he loved her, but really, Alys had no idea what their relationship was like. She'd met Brooke a couple of times, but she didn't know much about her future daughter-in-law.

It startled her now, though, to see her ex-sister-in-law throw her arms around her son and even more so, to see the way Ledge returned the hug and held on. Ledger—all the kids—had always been close with Claire and Josh, but the desperation in that hug, the look of raw need on his face was like a shard of glass poking in her throat. Still trying to process the way that hurt, *why* it hurt, Alys must have said something or made a noise of distress when Brooke hugged Claire just as enthusiastically as Ledger did. Fletch walked beside her, but suddenly, he was close enough that she felt the heat from his body. He slipped his arm around her shoulders and gave her upper arm a gentle squeeze.

"Are they close?" she whispered before she could stop herself. When Fletch hesitated, she peeked up at him as they crossed the hotel lobby to join the welcome wagon. Fletch looked pained, like he was afraid he would hurt her, but eventually, he gave her a quick nod. No explanation. No time for any explanation as suddenly, Alys and Fletch stood with the group and Ledger turned to them with a polite smile.

"Hey, Dad." Ledger shook Fletcher's hand, and the smile tipped more toward a happy grin. But it cooled again when he met Alys' eyes. "Mom."

"Ledger." She nodded and stepped toward him to hug him. Duty, but the need to touch him, to feel the solid presence of her son under her arms drove her toward him. He had to lean over to hug her, the same as he had Claire, but he didn't pull her in close. Alys swallowed the hurt and circled her arms around his shoulders. He was hard, muscular male under her arms, and he smelled like cedarwood and patchouli. Was the scent something he had chosen for himself or something Brooke liked on him?

Alys forced the thought away and patted Ledger's arm as he stepped back from her. She had a flash of a science fair years and years ago, when Ledger did a huge experiment with household cleaners and collected pages of data. She had stayed up late with him for nights on end, perfecting his presentation board, and in the end, Ledger got an A, but a classmate got a blue ribbon for her display and data collection on women's cologne. Alys figured the cologne study beat Ledger out because it was more interesting. Ledge had been crushed, but a hug from Alys and ice cream on the way home had been enough to cheer him up.

Jade had strep throat, so she missed the science fair completely. Fletch had stayed at home with her and worked on her project that she still had to turn in for a grade.

"Alys." Brooke offered her another version of the cool polite smile Ledger had given her.

"Brooke, you look lovely." She meant it. Her son's fiancée was a beautiful girl with high cheekbones, dazzling green eyes, and soft, flowing brunette waves.

"Thank you." Brooke stepped in and hugged Alys, but it was so quick, she didn't have time to process how stiff it was.

When Brooke stepped back, she gripped Alys' hands. "We're so glad you could be here."

Never mind that Alys hadn't talked to her son in ages, Brooke's comment was a slap in the face. Something a bride-to-be might say to a distant relative or a professional colleague, not her future mother-in-law. Alys managed a small nod, because people were watching them, and yes, she was the one who had left, so technically, she deserved any cold shoulder she got over the next several days.

But that didn't make it any easier to swallow.

A drink would help. She folded her arms over her chest when Brooke turned to Fletcher, relieved to see that he didn't appear to be any closer to the girl than she was. What kind of mother leaves her child and then has the nerve to be jealous of his relationship with his aunt?

"Hi, Alys."

More faces to greet. Brooke's parents—Julia and Roark. Alys had met them once before. They were probably good people, but they had probably heard more bad than good about her. Which made Alys defensive before either of them had opened their mouths that time.

"It's so nice to see you."

She could do this. Just channel that professional veneer. Even if she had to wear that mask for the rest of the vacation, until the wedding was over. Go through the motions and get back home.

The reminder that she had a home, a life separate from this hoopla, brought a stroke of calm. She gulped a deep breath when she felt her chest expand. She had the house Iva had left her. Plenty of space for now. Eventually, she would sell it. She had enough to live on, and she had a job, so she didn't need Iva's fortunes. But she would sell the house when she was ready and donate the money to cancer research, all in Iva's name.

The sunroom at the house was Iva's favorite room. Alys favored the library, but Iva loved the view of her flower garden from the sunroom. They'd spent so many mornings and evenings there together. Often, they didn't have to talk. Iva read self-help books and made notes for a book she wanted to publish before she died. Unfortunately, that hadn't happened. Alys had half a mind to dig in and organize the notes Iva did have and see if she could put something together to be published posthumous. She hadn't been able to give the woman what she needed when she was living; Alys wanted desperately to give her something now.

She realized they were moving, en masse, the whole group meandering through the lobby, down the hall, and to the patio doors. Fletch walked beside her, slowed with her when she did. She wanted to drag her feet. To slip away unnoticed. Find a dark bar. Even if she had to take the rental car and find a seedy bar somewhere far away from the resort, she would do it.

"You okay?" Fletch's deep voice wrapped around her comfortably, like a familiar, worn blanket.

"I can't do this."

"You can." He nodded. "This is your son. He's only going to get married once."

"Unless he and Brooke fuck up their marriage like we did, and then maybe he'll get married two or three more times."

"Allie."

She waited for him to remind her she had been the one to break up their marriage, but he surprised her and let that comment go.

"I can't go to lunch today. And tomorrow. And the next day and dinner tonight and tomorrow. I can't do this, Fletcher. I cannot sit at some table with these people and pretend that I'm okay. That I'm happy."

"Allie, we have to do this," he said gently. "Lunch today. Maybe dinner tonight. You don't have to be at their sides every day. But today is important, okay? I'll be right by your side."

Alys blinked up at him and stopped walking. Was his promise to be at her side supposed to make her feel better? A part of her wanted to laugh at his audacity; she'd left him. They had both moved on. Fletcher and his grief and his expectations and his love had been a huge part of the burden that had driven her away.

But she felt better. Marginally, but better. She might be drowning in emotions she didn't want to acknowledge, but Fletch was struggling right there with her.

"Take a deep breath."

Whether it was his calm voice or his bold, steady gaze, Alys wanted to listen to him. She needed an ally—which was ridiculous, but she couldn't deny it—and Fletch was standing with her now, holding her hands and telling her he would get her through the day.

The lively conversation faded away as their group moved further on without them. Out here under the sun, with all the blue sky and the darker blue ocean surrounding her, it was easier to breathe. Eyes still locked with his, Alys parted her lips and drew in a long, deep breath.

"Better?"

She nodded.

"I'll buy you a drink."

His offer made her laugh, and the soft sound was so real, it hurt.

"Okay."

He let go of her hands as they turned to catch up with the rest of the gang. A rush of sadness engulfed her, but this time it was all about Fletcher. His warm, capable hands. Before the divorce, they held hands all the time. She peeked at him now, and when she found his gaze fixed on the ocean, she looked at his hand and considered reaching for it.

She couldn't, though. The family might read things into that simple act. Fletcher might read things into it, too. And after that kiss last night, Alys couldn't let herself give Flech the wrong idea.

Howie's again, though everything about it felt different in the daytime. Rather than shadowed memories and heartache, today it felt beachy and fun. A Jimmy Buffet song hovered in the air as they all chose seats. Alys hung back, repulsed at the idea of having to sit down and make conversation with a table full of people.

She found herself seated between Fletch and Claire, and though it's what she wanted, she was a little disconcerted that Claire was sitting by Brooke. It was bad enough that Claire had apparently swooped in to mother Ledger. The idea that she and Brooke were close made her stomach hurt a little bit.

Fletch draped his arm over the back of her chair, though he was careful not to get too close. A spike of gratitude whirled with frustration inside her. He was sending out the signal that they were okay, they were friendly, and Alys was totally emotionally capable of being here. While she appreciated that, she wondered if he was keeping score. What would she owe him when this was over?

He spoke to Josh and Ledge across the table. Alys studied the flyer on the table with today's lunch specials and wondered how she was supposed to chew and swallow anything when her stomach was wrecked with nerves. To her right, Claire, Brooke, and Julia were already deep in conversation about a screw up with the flowers that had happened at a shower Brooke's girlfriends had thrown for her. Alys had been invited; she hadn't gone, because she was afraid to leave Iva alone.

"What do you want to drink?" Fletch leaned in so close when he spoke, his breath tickled her ear. "I don't know your poison."

While two fingers of something high enough proof to knock her on her ass sounded appealing, she couldn't hit the hard stuff over lunch in present company. She answered Fletch with a tiny shake of her head.

"Beer?" he suggested. Maybe it was because she moved—a little involuntary shiver when she felt his warm breath on her skin—but this time, Fletch's lips brushed the shell of her ear. She nodded silently, praying he didn't notice the sharp breath she took at his touch. "Okay."

He smoothed his fingers over her back, but before she could snap at him, he rested his hand on her chair. She turned her face toward him and watched him talk to Ledger, wondering if it hurt him the way it would hurt her to do so.

When their waitress approached them, the table fell quiet in sections, and Alys listened as everyone ordered their drinks.

She sat with her lips closed when Fletch ordered her beer and ignored the look Claire gave her.

"How's work?"

She looked up at Ledge's question, a little surprised to find him looking at her.

"It's good," she said simply. "Staying busy, so I can't complain. How about you?"

He answered with a half-hearted shrug. "I got laid off about three months ago."

"Really?" She flinched, guilt squeezing her throat closed. It wasn't her fault he was laid off, but as his mother, she should have known it happened. She wondered if Claire knew. "I can't believe downsizing at your plant would affect the engineering department."

"It did," he mumbled. "Low man on the totem pole gets the ax."

"I think the whole company is going under," Claire announced, confirming Alys' suspicions that she knew about the layoff.

"I'm working in oil exploration now, but I don't love that my job might be dependent on the political trends."

"But you could get to do some overseas travel," Claire pointed out in a tone that suggested they'd had the conversation before.

"I know." Ledger nodded, but he didn't appear happy.

"Kind of hard to start a marriage if he's traveling overseas and Brooke's back here in the states."

Claire gave Alys a harsh look. "It would be, but Brooke has looked into nursing abroad, too."

Stung by Claire's intimate knowledge of their plans and by the thought of her son leaving the country for any length of time, Alys simply nodded.

"That's great," she said quietly.

The waitress arrived with their drinks; Alys counted to ten before picking her bottle up and taking a drink. No need to put on a show and give Brooke's family something else to talk about. She had no doubt they had all whispered when she moved in with Iva.

"What're you doing tomorrow?" Fletch leaned close to her again, but he was careful not to nudge her ear this time. Around them, conversation buzzed, and lunches were ordered. Alys hated the warmth she felt inside at Fletch's direct gaze, the quiet murmur meant only for her.

"Nothing." She shook her head, asked for a Caesar chicken wrap when it was her turn to order, and sipped her beer. Fletch ordered fish tacos, which naturally brought back a memory of a dinner on another trip, this one to San Diego.

"Want to go golfing?"

She would go to the pool, but she might run into Claire again. Or worse—Brooke and her entourage. But golfing? Did she want to spend a day on the course? The idea of going alone tempted her. But she didn't have a tee time, and at a resort like this, she couldn't just show up and think she would play tomorrow.

Before she could answer him, Fletch tipped his head and let his eyes roam over her face. He brushed his thumb over her back again.

"With me. You could go with me. I have a tee time."

"You want me to play golf with you?" she asked with a frown.

"Josh had planned to go, but he and Claire are going on a daytrip somewhere." Fletch plucked his pint glass from the table and stared at it for a moment. "But yes, Allie. I want you to golf with me tomorrow."

She wanted to say no. She wasn't here to do fun things with Fletch. But being out on the golf course with him was a good excuse not to be with Brooke and her family. And it sounded social, which was definitely a plus.

"Okay." She spoke quietly, but she saw the flash of happiness in Fletcher's eyes, so she knew he heard her.

After lunch, the group broke up. Claire was headed to the pool; Alys heard Brooke and her mother discussing it. When Claire asked her to come along, Alys begged off. She claimed she needed to check in with work, when in reality, she needed space. Solitude. Lunch had been a two-hour long ordeal, and she was exhausted from playing polite, and it was all she could do to not run back through the resort to get to the Valentine Suite.

She worried that Fletch might follow her, but he didn't. Maybe he had plans. Maybe he was spending time with Ledger. Or maybe, he had read that panic that had climbed her throat and into her eyes by the time Brooke's parents paid the bill. Whatever the reason, Alys was grateful for the reprieve. She had four hours to herself. A nap. A hot soak in the luxurious tub in the suite. Some reading on the balcony. Anything in the world she could do alone would be perfect to rest up for the next round.

Cocktails at six. Dinner at seven.

Chapter Ten

BROOKE'S RING WAS NOTHING LIKE ALYS' WEDDING ring, but it reminded her of it, nonetheless. Brooke's diamond was offset with sapphires and channel diamonds in the yellow gold band. Alys' was a two carat round cut diamond and two diamond eternity bands. She hadn't worn it since she filed for divorce, but she found herself rubbing her thumb under her ring finger quite often while she stood next to Claire and Brooke at the hotel bar.

The quiet strains of piano music were the perfect backdrop to the evening. In fact, Alys supposed they looked quite happy, all of them gathered at the bar, dressed for a night out, sipping cocktails from Tom Collins and Old-Fashioned glasses. Though she didn't mean to, she kept tabs on Fletch. She didn't want to care where he was, who he was talking to, but her eyes were constantly drawn to him.

He wore a white button down with dark wash jeans. Alys recognized the jeans; she had bought them for him. She loved the way denim molded his thighs and his butt and everything else that she shouldn't be thinking about tonight. Though he was making the rounds, he glanced at her from time to time, as if he needed to know where she was, too.

"What're you doing tomorrow, Alys?" Brooke asked her now. Alys said a silent prayer of thanks that Fletch had asked her to golf with him.

"Golfing with Fletch."

"Oh." Her future daughter-in-law's smile was as honest as Alys' was fake. "That sounds like fun. Have you played recently?"

She and Fletch used to play eighteen holes nearly every day they could, when their schedules aligned. Most likely, Brooke knew that through Ledger.

"No, I haven't played in quite a while," Alys admitted. She offered the girl a rueful grin. "Fletch will probably mop the floor with me."

"Ledger's trying to teach me to play." Brooke arched her eyebrows as if to indicate it wasn't going well.

"You should take lessons," Alys suggested. Over Brooke's shoulder, she saw Fletch meander away from Roark, only to enter into conversation with Josh.

"That's what Ledge says." Brooke nodded.

Alys sipped at her Old-Fashioned, wishing it was straight whiskey. By the time Fletch made his way around the group, they were walking again. This time to Calliope, yet another upscale seafood restaurant on the resort. Alys walked side by side with Claire, feeling a bit like Bill Murray in *Groundhog Day*.

Once back in the Valentine Suite earlier, she had chucked her pale-yellow linen capris and slid between the sheets. She wasn't particularly sleepy, but she was bone tired. Exhausted from sleeping in a tight tense bundle at night, careful not to get close to Fletch. Drained from being social earlier at lunch. A headache pounded through her brain, so it was a wonder she managed to fall asleep. She woke in the same position she laid down in, on her back, one leg bent so her foot touched her knee.

Well-rested, she had still been slow to climb from the cocoon of sleep. A peek at her phone told her she'd slept almost two hours. From the bed, she trailed into the bathroom, stripping the rest of her clothing off to relax in the tub for a while.

Dinner was good; she hadn't believed it was possible, but she was hungry. Tucked between Fletch and Josh this time, she sipped a glass of chardonnay and worked on a tuna steak that was prepared perfectly. Fletch ate fettucine with scallops in a spicy pink sauce. When he held his fork out to her offering her a bite, she took it without thinking. When dinner was over, and the bill paid, she lingered with everyone else, over another drink. She hadn't contributed much to any conversation, but she was listening to Fletch and Josh talk, and she decided she preferred their voices to the quiet of the suite.

Even when the sun dipped low enough to slip into the ocean, and the evening air grew cooler, Alys was comfortable at the table. She watched Brooke and her friends drag Ledger to the dance floor, and the emotions in her belly warred with her dinner. It was almost thrilling to see her son surrounded by pretty girls, smiling and talking like he didn't have a care in the world. But unless he was inhuman, he did have a care, and that niggled at Alys, making her neck and her shoulders hurt.

She stewed over it, letting her mind wander for the first time in a long time, to what Ledger was thinking, how he dealt with his grief. Surely, he still had moments of uncontrollable grief.

Jade was his twin. And even if he hadn't been particularly close to Kase, Alys had to assume he still missed him. Fletch kept up his end of the conversation with Josh—they had moved from robotics to the new Ford Bronco. By then, Alys made no effort to follow the conversation, so she had no idea how they had jumped subjects. She pretended not to notice Fletch's hand occasionally touching her back. He wasn't coming on to her; he was simply trying to comfort her. Between his touch and the appearance of a full wine glass each time hers was nearly empty, Alys was almost startled to realize she was content to sit there beside him.

"What're we doing?" She roused herself from her thoughts when Fletch took her hand and tugged her gently from her chair. A peek around the table told her some of their group had either ditched the activities or joined the kids on the dance floor. Roark and Josh sat on the opposite side of the table in animated conversation.

"Dance with me." Fletch's voice, smooth as silk, and the wine she had consumed made it impossible to argue. But she trailed behind him, stiff when he turned to take her in his arms.

Rather than look up at him or tip her head down to rest on his shoulder, Alys kept her eyes trained a bit to the right.

"Why are we dancing?" she finally asked him. The song playing wasn't one of her favorites. As far as she knew, Fletch didn't love it. It had no significant meaning to them.

"Because Ledge is dancing with his bride-to-be, and I wanted to dance."

"It feels wrong," she mumbled.

Fletch moved his hands a bit, from her hips to her waist, as if she meant dancing with him felt physically wrong.

"Doing okay?" he asked quietly.

"Mmm." She melted a bit and sank into him, telling herself it was the wine. Too much. So much that she regretted agreeing to golf with him in the morning. Another slow song started, and this one, "When a Man Loves a Woman" hurt a little. Fletch gathered her closer when she gave in and rested her head on his shoulder. Rather than watch others dance, rather than get that occasional glimpse of Josh and Roark still at their table, Alys closed her eyes. They hardly moved now, swaying gently to the music. It was dangerous to be this close to him, but she couldn't peel herself off him. The wine and the movement now made her dizzy, but the true danger lie in what Fletch was thinking.

She took a step back when the music changed this time. "Long Cool Woman in a Black Dress" didn't lend itself to slow dancing, and they shared far too many memories of dancing and drinking at parties and receptions, and Alys worried now that she might be sick. But before she could dart away, Claire and Josh joined them, and suddenly, they were dancing together—all four of them.

And if Alys still had a heart capable of being happy, this might have been okay.

As if he sensed her reluctance, Fletch stayed at her side. He handed her another glass of wine, but he also offered her water, which she drank with greed. She wasn't drunk, but still, she knew she was under the influence because she wouldn't dream of something so outrageous as dancing if she weren't.

Losing Jade and Kase had sucked her soul dry. While she had found something with Iva, Alys had been destroyed by that time, and she lived by memory, going through the motions when her heart didn't care anymore.

"I haven't heard this song since Hallie played it on repeat the entire year she turned thirteen." Claire leaned close to Alys and hollered over the music. Alys knew the song—another in a long stretch of hip-hop dance songs—but she couldn't say she remembered Hallie listening to it on repeat all year. Then again, her own kids had done the same and more, so it wasn't like she would remember everything.

She noticed Ledger with his arms around Brooke, barely swaying to the music. Pressed together from chests to hips, they seemed oblivious to everyone around them. Alys catalogued the intimacy between them, their eyes locked and smiles mirroring each other's.

"When was the last time you danced?"

Claire's question drew Alys' attention from her son. She met Claire's eyes briefly, but uncomfortable with her ex-sister-in-law's bold curiosity, she turned her face again, refusing to admit even to herself that she was looking for Fletch.

"Probably the last time I was here, Claire," she mumbled. Despite the loud music and the noise of the crowd, Claire answered with a simple nod.

"Not with Iva?"

Alys tipped her head at Claire and turned her back to Fletch and Josh.

"I thought we talked about this."

Claire took her hands and gave her a gentle yank closer. Still dancing, Fletch couldn't know Alys was ready to be rescued.

"You and I used to share everything. I miss that." Claire leaned in and spoke loudly. "I told you about me and Josh and Andrew Jones."

"That was twenty-five years ago," Alys answered. "And whatever did happen between me and Iva wasn't like that."

"Whatever did...happen..." Claire drew back and stared at Alys. Rather than look giddy and greedy for details, she looked hurt. "So, something did happen."

"There was kissing, Claire." Alys shrugged. "We slept in the same bed, but that doesn't mean we were scissoring—"

"Scissoring?" Claire yelped. Alys looked around, wondering if Josh and Fletch heard her bitter laugh.

"Look, Iva was honest with me from the beginning. I knew she was bisexual, but we were friends. She said she had feelings for me. I didn't have those same feelings, and Iva was okay with that."

"Have you been with anyone? Since Fletch?"

"No."

"Does it bother you? That Fletch was with Trish?"

Of course it did, but how was Alys supposed to admit that and not invite a million other questions from Fletch's sister?

"I get it. You left him, blah blah blah." Claire had stopped moving now, so Alys did, too. She looked around again for Fletch, surprised that he wasn't within her sights. Claire took her hand, and like a million times through the years when they had been not just sisters-in-law but the best of friends, Alys followed her. She doubted she would be comfortable discussing whatever Claire brought up, especially not Fletch and Trish, but Alys was startled to realize she trusted Claire. Even if she dug in with both hands and ripped Alys' heart out, she wasn't trying to hurt her.

"I have a headache," she mumbled. Probably too much wine, but the music was louder than anything she'd heard since her world had changed, and no doubt, that added to it.

"Does it bother you at all, Allie?" Claire stopped walking at an elaborate flowerbed, though darkness had fallen and only a small portion of the vivid reds and yellows was visible now in the landscaping lighting. "To think about Fletch with another woman?"

"I have no claim to Fletcher anymore."

"But does it hurt? I think about it with Josh sometimes. I don't think I could stand it."

Alys folded her arms over her chest and tipped her head at Claire. "Why? Why would you ever think about that with Josh?"

Claire shook her head and waved Alys' questions away.

"Is something going on with you two?"

"No," Claire insisted, though Alys wondered if her answer was too quick. "No. I mean, we fight now and then. Hallie's situation has made things tense."

"Was she raped?"

"She doesn't know," Claire answered simply. "Odds are, yes."

"Does Josh have someone else?"

"No. No, of course not. I just...when we fight now, with the whole thing with Hallie, I just catch myself wondering worst case scenario. And I think about you and Fletch, and how..."

"How I bailed when life got hard," Alys supplied a line for her and shrugged off the tension when Claire met her eyes.

"Goddammit, Alys." She sighed. "Do you know how hard it is to make friends at our age? You left my brother. Okay, whatever. No, I don't get it. But you left me, too. I went for coffee with Eleanor Grady a few times. The woman makes me crazy. I went out for drinks with Heidi Laughlin and Ginger Paxton a few times."

Alys took her words like a sucker punch in her belly. She sucked in a sharp breath and looked away, but not before Claire noticed.

"They're fun," she said quietly. "You're close to Heidi."

"Yeah, but they're not you." Claire pushed her fingers back through her hair. "It sucks, doesn't it? You don't like knowing I have other friends."

"Claire."

"And you were sleeping with your new friend."

Alys barked a harsh laugh and rolled her eyes. "You wanna sleep with me? How about you and Fletch swap rooms?"

"What did I do? Why did you cut me out of your life, too?"

"Maybe because you're Fletcher's sister? Because you're just as close to the situation as he is. Because I was drowning in grief, Claire. His. Yours. Everybody's grief but my own. I had to walk out to save myself."

"That's not true. That's not fair!" Claire snapped. "I was there for you. I did everything I could for you and Fletch."

"I know." Alys nodded. "I do know that. And I know you don't believe me, but I appreciate everything you did. The fact that you're there for Fletch. That you're tight with Ledge and Brooke—"

Claire licked her lips, drawing Alys' attention. Her tears now irritated Alys as much as they had just after the accident.

"You didn't wanna mother him." Claire spoke calmly. "Someone had to."

Alys didn't bother to hide the way Claire's words cut her this time.

"That hurts." Her voice was hushed, so much emotion in her chest and her throat, it hurt to breathe. "And yes, Claire, to answer your question it hurts to think about Fletch with anyone else."

"There you are."

Claire stiffened at the sound of Josh's words. Alys swallowed hard, hoping to get herself under control before she ended up face to face with Fletch.

"What're you two doing?" Josh appeared from the direction of the restaurant patio and draped his arm around Claire's shoulders.

"Just talking," Claire said simply.

"Need anything?" Fletch stood close to Alys, but he didn't touch her. She wondered how he knew better. Earlier tonight, he had been attentive with small touches, just a brush of her arm or shoulder, as if he was grounding her, reminding her to breathe. Now, he seemed to sense that touching her would send her scrambling to get away from him.

"No." Arms still folded over her chest, she glanced at him and found his face a mix of concern and sadness. "I think I'm ready to call it a night."

"Okay." He nodded.

"You don't have to, Fletch. I'll be fine."

"No, it's okay." His lopsided grin was boyish and charming. Alys had to look away to keep images of Trish kissing him, kissing that sweet grin out of her head.

"I'm ready, too," Claire announced with a glance at Josh.

"Me, too. I'm beat," he agreed.

Alys dropped her arms to her sides as they walked, hyperaware of Fletch walking at her side. Of his hand so close to hers she could link her fingers with his if she wanted to.

She didn't. Instead, she jammed her hands in the pockets of her jeans and tipped her head down. Josh and Fletch spent the walk over the campus and across the lobby talking about a mutual friend's golf game. She and Claire didn't speak, but Alys couldn't help but notice Claire's finger hooked through Josh's belt loop. She used to do that with Fletch.

Once they said goodnight at a fork in the hallway, Alys remembered a lot of things she used to do with Fletch. Curling up together on the sofa to watch TV. Lounging on the patio with hot coffee or a glass of wine. Walking at a local park on summer evenings. Waking in the middle of the night and turning to each other to make love.

"You okay?" he asked as they made their way to the end of the hall and took a left. He pulled his key card from his pocket to wave at the sensor on the door and peeked at her. "Looked kind of intense out there."

She wasn't sure she was okay, but the last damned thing she wanted to do at the moment was talk about Claire.

"I'm fine," she mumbled. When he raised his eyebrows as if to argue, she shook her head and gestured at the door. Fletch studied her face a moment longer and pushed the door open. Maid service had been in to turn the bed down, which was ridiculous, even more so because nothing romantic was happening in that bed. They'd left a lamp on in the living area, so they stood in shadows in the foyer, rather than darkness.

Rather than hurry to the bedroom, Alys watched Fletch turn and engage the deadbolt and the chain lock. He stood with his back to her for a moment, sighed, and lifted his hands to unbutton his shirt.

"Fletch."

He turned, apparently surprised she hadn't moved.

"Allie."

She might want to blame him, but they moved at the same time. Fletch dropped his hands to grab her upper arms, and Alys took over with the buttons of his shirt. She pressed up on her tiptoes to kiss him, shoving the broadcloth over his shoulders, irritated that he wore a gray dri-fit shirt under it.

Fletch leaned into her kiss, his tongue sliding and dancing over hers, fingers clutching her arms as if he were afraid she would vanish. Alys dropped the shirt to the floor and closed her fingers around the back of his neck. Heat radiated through his shirt; his skin was hot under her fingers. She tasted wine on his lips and his tongue, and she heard words, memories, he didn't say out loud in the way he breathed when he broke the kiss and nuzzled her face with his nose.

She didn't want tender.

Desperation, the same-old sobering grief roared through her blood like fire. Either she needed to devour him or claw a hole in her throat so she could breathe. Hungry, harsh, Alys turned her face with his and lunged for him, claiming his mouth in another kiss. No finesse, all need, her teeth cracked against his, his upper lip caught between them. Fletch groaned and let go of her arms to cup her ass with the same frenzied desperation.

Alys lifted her legs to circle his waist, just as Fletch backed her up to press her against the wall. His erection pressed hard and hot at her middle. Alys tilted her hips to rub over him, drawing a string of muttered dirty words from his lips. She caught *fuck* and *need* and *wet* on her tongue and licked her lips and stopped for just a second to look him in the eyes.

"Are you sure?"

"Yes."

She was. Instead of waiting on him to undress her, she lowered her legs to the floor, unbuttoned her jeans, and kicked out of them and her wedge sandals. Fletch watched with hooded eyes. She shook her head when he reached for the hem of her shirt.

"Fuck me, Fletch." She hooked her fingers in her panties and shoved them down over her hips. His hands were hot and rough under her thighs when she lifted her legs around his waist again. He kissed her, this time his mouth assaulting hers. Alys moaned and nodded, hands at his waist, tugging his belt from his jeans.

"Jesus, Allie," he panted when she parted his zipper and reached to take him in her hand.

"Make it hurt, Fletch."

She didn't have to ask twice. Fletch yanked her hips forward as he drove into her, her shoulders slamming and almost digging into the wall at her back. Thick and hard, he filled her and then pulled out immediately to pound inside her again.

"You need more." He grunted the words into her neck, because always when they made love, she had to have his touch, his fingers on her core to come.

"No." She squeezed her eyes closed. Unable to bear the thought of him touching her there, touching her intimately to make her come instead of making her hurt, she slipped her own hand between their bodies and worked the tight nub of sensitive skin as Fletch continued to hammer her against the wall.

"I'm gonna come, Al."

She opened her eyes to find him watching her face.

"Just come, Fletcher," she gasped.

"Allie!" He might have shouted, but he dipped his head again and sank his teeth into her neck. He strained against her, his cock still hard and hot inside her. Alys squeezed him, milking his pleasure, but working frantically to take her own. Her fingers slid in a frenzy over that magical spot, until finally, she shattered there between Fletch and the wall.

She chanted *fuck*, *fuck*, *fuck* over and over, not moving her hand, not stopping, and Fletch still hard enough inside her to press the good spots, continued to pump his hips against her.

Suddenly aware that she was no longer chanting fuck, but a different F word, *one far worse*, she bit her lip and rested her forehead on his shoulder. She breathed in ragged panting, Fletcher's hot, wet breath on her neck as he did the same chasing a chill over her skin.

"You okay?"

"Don't ask me that, okay?" She kissed him full on the mouth again. "Just don't."

"I get that this didn't mean anything, Allie." His voice was low and tight with anger. "But I need to know if you're okay."

"I'm fine."

Lie.

She lowered her legs again as Fletch eased out of her. Empty and cold, she watched him tug his jeans back up and button them.

"You can have the bathroom first." He turned away from her to pick up his shirt from the floor.

Even though she had slept with him for years, even though he had just been buried balls deep inside her, she couldn't stand the idea of prancing around naked before him. So, she scooped up her panties and stepped into them quickly, glad now for the shadows.

Fletch disappeared to the balcony when she went to the bathroom. She showered quickly, though there was a small part of her that hated to wash away what they had just done. Her lips were swollen; her face whisker burnt, when she studied herself in the mirror and brushed her teeth.

Awake when Fletch came to bed, she stared up at the ceiling in the darkness.

"Did you use protection with her?" she finally whispered.

"Yes."

She breathed a sigh of relief. Wished she could tell him goodnight. Wished she could kiss him. Softly, this time. Tenderly. Instead, she turned her back to him and closed her eyes.

Chapter Eleven

WHEN SHE AND FLETCH PLAYED GOLF BEFORE THEY were divorced, the quiet in the early mornings on the course was peaceful, almost reverent. Today was quiet, but Alys wasn't sure that had anything to do with reverence. Maybe it was regret. Neither of them had said a word this morning when Fletch's alarm went off, though Alys had considered bailing. But he slipped out of bed quickly, only to disappear into the kitchen and make coffee. The smell of it brewing destroyed her resolve and dragged her out of bed while he was in the shower.

She sipped a cup while in the kitchen, butt parked against the counter, arms folded over her chest. Stupid to waste a morning in a kitchen smaller and less appealing than hers at home when she could be on the balcony with the ocean view, but she lingered for several moments. Thinking about the night before. Dinner and drinks. Dancing. God, she hated that. The memories gutted her now. The vibration of the bass in her breastbone. The way she had moved her hips. The carefree dance steps. The smile on her face.

Singing along to the songs she liked the best.

What would Jade and Kase think if they knew she had gone out last night and enjoyed herself? She didn't just enjoy herself, though. Last night was probably the most fun she'd allowed herself since the accident.

And then there was Fletch. What the hell had she been thinking?

She didn't get too far into those regrets there in the kitchen, though. Because Fletch himself appeared, dressed and ready to go, to grab coffee. Their eyes had met, but Alys had slipped out of the room quickly and ducked into the shower to avoid conversation.

Even now, on the third hole, sharing a golf cart, they hadn't done much but mumble or grunt to each other. Almost like married couples communicate, except in a different tone. Alys sipped a bottle of water as she watched Fletch tee up on the par 5 hole. She eyed his muscular legs and his ass, remembering the way she had mauled him last night. Kissing him. Coming onto him. Reaching into his pants to touch him. The desperate need for him to fill her.

She had hoped he would hurt her enough to drive her demons out. Sex after losing Jade and Kase had been animalistic and violent, but in Alys' case, it had been about fighting and trying hard to use him to drive that pain away. Maybe last night she had the crazy idea that she could make him want to use her, to hurt her, and maybe his desperation would drive the pain away.

It had.

For those minutes he was deep inside her, drilling into her and banging her shoulders and her hips on the wall, Alys was steeped in pleasure and sex and skin and Fletch. She hadn't wanted his hands on her; she needed to control that part of it, but he had delivered with everything else.

The moment passed though. The second he pulled out of her and stepped away. The cold air on her wet skin had been a cruel reminder of where they were, who they were to each other now, and why they clawed at each other rather than stroking with love.

When they went to bed, she wanted more of him, with him. Not the frenzied fucking against the wall, but something tender. Sweet. Soft kisses and gentle hands. She wanted him to make love to her, because if hard, dirty sex only took the pain away for seconds at a time, maybe making love would deliver a peace that lasted longer.

Needing him that way scared her.

His tee shot was as beautiful as his swing. Alys made sure to shift her attention to the ball as it sailed over the fairway. She couldn't be caught watching him, not after last night. Apparently, not happy with where he ended up, Fletch came back to the cart with a frown on his face. He muttered something and dropped his driver back into his bag as she climbed out of the cart.

Would he watch her the way she watched him? Did he regret last night? After all, when it was done, he made that comment about what happening not meaning anything. His words had stung, and not only because if someone was going to say it, she wanted it to be her. But what if it hurt a little because she *wanted* it to mean something?

She pulled the driver from her rented bag of clubs. She'd bogeyed the first hole and shot par on the second, but this was a par five, so she needed a long drive. Alys wasn't sure she had it in her, and she didn't love the rented clubs, either. She wasn't up for excuses, though. It had been a long time since she had golfed; no way was her game going to look anything but rusty.

"Did you put sunscreen on?" Fletch asked as she turned away from the cart.

"What?"

"Did you?" he asked with a shrug when she glanced back at him.

"Yes."

"Because you always think you'll be fine, and you always burn." He shrugged.

"I did." She rolled her eyes and leaned over to stick her tee in the ground.

"Lip stuff?"

"Fletch," she snapped. "Yes."

It irked her that he knew her so well, that he was tending to her like she was a little kid instead of a grown woman who had lost a huge part of her life. He was quiet as she took a couple of practice swings.

It was because of Claire.

That ravenous need for Fletch last night. Claire had been picking at the scabs Alys had grown over all the pain—losing the kids, the divorce, the Jeffries threatening a lawsuit because Kase had been drinking, losing Iva—since they'd first bumped into each other out here. It wasn't any one thing. It wasn't the situation with Hallie. Or Claire's insane curiosity about Alys and Iva. Or even Claire's nosy question about how Alys honestly felt about Fletch having another woman.

It was the dancing. The wine. The laughing. Because even though Alys had succumbed to the peer pressure to stay on the floor and dance with all of them, she had sworn to herself she wouldn't enjoy it. She had said a silent promise, like a prayer, to Jade and Kase, to Iva even, that she wouldn't enjoy it. That she would do whatever it took to get through the night, but she wouldn't have fun.

Claire and Josh were fun. She and Fletch had spent far too much of their lives hanging out—in good times and bad—with them for her to feign disinterest in them now. And if she felt that way about Claire and Josh, how in the hell was she supposed to escape from this vacation and Fletch, without losing her heart—again—in the process?

She swung her arms in a perfect arc and drove the ball in a bit of a slice. Lowering the driver, she watched the shot so she could easily find her ball.

"Your clubface was open," Fletch told her when she returned to the cart. She eyed him silently and dropped her driver back in the bag.

"Are you playing with Ledger while you're here?" She plopped down in the cart and held on when Fletch tapped the gas pedal.

"Yes."

She avoided his eyes as he drove and devoured the beauty of the course. She and Iva used to walk in Iva's neighborhood; her rambling old house was close to the city course. Iva didn't play, but she loved to meander around the perimeter of the course and drink it all in.

"Did you know about Hallie?" Alys asked Fletch without looking his way.

"Yeah." He sighed. "Bad deal."

"Why didn't you tell me?"

"Really?" His chuckle was cold and sarcastic. "The last time I called you to ask you about signing some paperwork with insurance, you came unglued."

"I didn't come unglued," she argued. "I was in the middle of fixing Iva's breakfast and asked if I could call you back."

"Josh said Hallie's coming in this week." Fletch chose to ignore the promise of a fight.

"Yeah. I just feel terrible for her. For Claire."

"Did you tell her that?"

Alys caught herself before she could answer him. Had she told Claire that?

"Have you seen her? Hallie?" She peeked at Fletch as he slowed the cart in the middle of the fairway. Alys' ball lay about twenty feet to their right.

"I saw her on her spring break," he said quietly. "She wasn't herself."

"I bet Josh would like to kill the guy."

"Of course he would," Fletch shrugged, "that's what dads with daughters want to do when they fail to protect their little girls."

Alys climbed out of the cart and looked back at Fletch. "It's not like it was Josh's fault."

"No, it wasn't," Fletch agreed. "But try telling Josh that."

Alys eyed the green from the cart.

"Seven iron?" She glanced at Fletch and grabbed it when he nodded his agreement. Fletch drove on to find his ball, staying well out of her way so she could take her next shot.

Did Josh think what happened to Hallie was his fault? Parents couldn't protect their children from everything. Hallie lived on a college campus, and she was surrounded by coeds. Some strangers. Some friends. Some she may have gone out with. And one of those guys had taken advantage of her. How could Josh have protected her from that?

How could Alys have protected Kase and Jade from a drunk driving accident?

It wasn't the same, though, was it? Kase, five years underage, was driving while intoxicated. His accident killed himself, his sister, and his girlfriend. Alys sized her shot up and tried to shrug off the guilt she still felt about what had happened.

This time her ball landed in a perfect position on the fairway. She took her time getting to it, a hand against the brim of her hat to shield the sun off her face as she watched Fletch swing again.

"Nice shot," he told her when they reached the cart at the same time.

"Thanks."

"What did Claire say to you?"

Alys stuck her club in the bag, grabbed her water bottle, and uncapped it.

"About Hallie?"

"Last night," Fletch corrected her. "You guys looked pretty intense when we found you."

She took a swig of water, wiped her mouth, and twisted the cap back on the bottle. It would be easy to lie. To blow off his question. He'd never know, because it wasn't likely Claire would bring any of it up with him.

Fletch looked at her in askance when she laughed softly.

"Well, your sister is dying for dirt about me and Iva."

The sharp look he gave her made her uncomfortable. Alys looked away when heat roared up from her belly to her neck and face.

"And she wanted to know if it bothered me that you were with Trish."

Before he could say a word, Alys grabbed a club and headed out for her next shot. She was still a ways from the green, but she would be okay if she kept her next shot on the fairway again. This time, it was hard to concentrate, though, because she felt Fletch's gaze on her like a heat ray. He was either imagining her with Iva now or thinking about the things he and Trish had done together. Neither option made her feel good.

She put the ball a bit to the right again and waited for Fletch to tell her what she did wrong. She always had the tendency to slice her drives, to leave her club face open. Fletch had already grabbed his next club and headed closer to the green for his next shot. Alys put her club away and jumped in the driver's seat.

His swing looked professional. Alys used to tease him, tell him he should wear the bright golf fashion Ricky Fowler preferred. Back in the good days, they would laugh about it. Fletch would sling his arm around her shoulders and draw her in like he was going to kiss her and then tickle her until she thought she would pee her pants.

They played the rest of the hole without conversation, Fletch with a par and Alys a double bogey. For the remainder of the outing, conversation regressed back to the mumbles and grunts about this shot or that, and Alys figured Fletch was thinking about Trish. Maybe he was in love with her. Maybe he should have given her a baby, so they would still be together.

The idea drove her straight to the ladies' room when they finished the eighteenth hole. She rushed away from him on trembling knees. She wasn't sick, but she did need a breather. A break from his constant presence. Alys felt like she'd been walking a tightwire for the past four hours, careful not to throw herself off it, and yet, oddly attracted to the freefall feeling that would surely steal her breath away if she did so.

When she emerged from the ladies' room, she found Fletch at a table on the patio. He had ordered her a beer. She felt a surge of irrational anger. He had lost the right to order for her, to speak for her, when they divorced. When he put his dick in another woman.

And yet, Alys had been the one to push him away, right to the other woman.

He didn't look up from his phone when she sat down. Alys took a long drink. The beer—it was a simple lager—was good and cold, so she decided to forgive him. She eyed him boldly while he studied his screen, muttering here and there, and finally put the phone down.

"I ordered you a salad," he told her. "With blackened salmon."

Another swell of anger, and again, because it wasn't fair that he knew her so well.

"Thanks." She nodded. "Talking to Trish?" Fletch arched his eyebrows in question, so Alys tipped her head at his phone. "Talking to Trish?"

"No." He took a deep breath and looked over her shoulder as if he couldn't bear to hold eye contact any longer.

"Do you love her, Fletch?"

"Asked and answered." He frowned, but he still wouldn't look at her.

"It's okay," she said softly. "If you do."

"It wouldn't bother you? If I told you I loved her?"

"It would," she admitted. "But I suppose I asked for it."

"You did," he agreed, "but no. I'm not in love with her, Allie. I like her. But it's not fair for me to keep her tied down."

"Do you hate me?" Her whisper was thick and heavy with regret.

"Sometimes," he said simply.

They lapsed into silence. Fletch seemed transfixed by whatever or whoever was behind her. Alys took a moment to look at her phone. She glanced at her email, but she had no desire to get mired in business issues at the moment. She made a show of putting her phone down, although it wasn't like Fletch could ask her if she was talking to Iva.

She eyed Fletch's plate when the waitress swooped in with their lunches. Fletch asked for another beer; Alys simply nodded when the girl looked at her in askance.

"What did you order?" She leaned forward to eye the sandwich.

"Grouper." He cut the whole thing in half and asked without looking at her, "do you want a bite?"

"Do you care?"

"Do you care if I care?" He shot her a look, the corner of his mouth creeping upward.

"No."

He handed her half of the sandwich and watched with interest when she took a bite. Their eyes locked as she chewed and handed the sandwich back to him. The sudden flare of heat between her legs left her breathless, and she gasped and covered her mouth, still full of food. Fletch looked away and sipped his beer.

"Do you think Hallie will be okay?" she asked once she had swallowed the grouper and washed it down with a drink.

"Did you tell Claire it would bother you?" Fletch asked at the same time.

"What?"

"When she asked you last night. About me and Trish."

Alys pursed her lips and nodded. "Yeah," she mumbled after a few moments of uncomfortable silence. "I did."

"She was a little lost without you," he spoke quietly, eyes on the table between them now. "At first."

Alys gave him a quick shrug when he glanced at her. At first. Maybe all of them had been a little lost without her. At first. Seemed like they had all moved on just fine without her.

"What's on your agenda tomorrow?"

"Nothing." She shook her head. "I think I might camp out on the balcony and get some work done. Things're gonna get crazy pretty quick with the rest of the wedding party showing up."

Alys dreaded the spa day most of all. In fact, she had half a mind to beg off and hole up in the suite. After all, they had all moved on without her, so no one needed her there.

Chapter Twelve

SHE DID HIDE OUT IN THE SUITE MONDAY MORNING. After another late-night dinner—though she drank considerably less and there was no dancing—she slept in a bit, ignoring Fletch when he got up and showered and left the suite early. A cool, lazy breeze nudged the curtains, and Alys lay for a while once she was fully awake, listening to the distant sound of the ocean.

Once she did get up, she made coffee and slipped out to the balcony with her laptop. As was always the case, she lost track of time and didn't shower until a few hours later. Restless, she took the rental out for a drive in the afternoon and ended up shopping a bit. Maybe because she felt guilty for dodging Claire today and maybe because she missed her, she found a beaded bracelet in the bold colors Claire favored and bought it for a gift. That idea drove her onward, through two more boutiques, and finally, she purchased gifts for Hallie and Brooke.

The gifts wouldn't make up for her general absence in their lives, most especially not for her absence in whatever today's events had been. But they made her feel a tiny bit better as she headed back to the resort.

She'd had them gift-wrapped, but she decided to wait another few days to deliver them. After all, Hallie wasn't even here yet. Fletch's voice carried through the living area as she headed to the bedroom to put the bags away. A glance at the French doors showed his bare feet propped up on the white wicker stool on the balcony. A tiny little flame licked up her inner thighs at the sight. Memories of waking next to him, his bare skin sliding over hers. Showering with him.

"Jesus, Alys," she hissed as she hurried on through the room to the bedroom.

Dinner tonight was up to each of them individually. Alys was grateful for that. She wasn't sure she could stomach yet another group dining experience. On the other hand, she cringed when she heard Fletch come inside, expecting him to ask her to go somewhere with him and Claire and Josh.

She held her breath, head resting on the chair on the bedroom balcony, eyes closed. She wouldn't tell him no, but pretending things were normal was exhausting. She would be an empty shell of a woman by the weekend at this rate. Because she wanted to know what Fletch was doing, she made herself sit still and not look back over her shoulder to find him. It sounded like he was rifling through his luggage. Maybe changing for dinner.

She heard the slide of the pocket door and wondered if he was going to shower. But only minutes later, the door opened, and she heard his footsteps again.

Where would they go tonight? Somewhere off the resort might be nice, but she wouldn't suggest it.

When another fifteen minutes had passed and Fletch hadn't stuck his head out the door to talk to her, Alys decided to find him. Hunger nipped at her belly, and if she were honest, she'd had enough solitude for the day.

The suite was empty. All the lights off, though the afternoon daylight was ample lighting for her to see. His wallet was gone from where she'd seen it on his nightstand. His phone, too. Stunned that he had gone out without her, she swallowed a mouthful of emotion and grabbed her own phone and credit card.

Dinner by the pool was peaceful, and part of her enjoyed it. She sipped a glass of Chardonnay and nibbled on a plate of pasta. There were two families in the water, a few other people relaxed in the deck chairs. When Alys was finished with her dinner, she sat on the edge of the pool with her feet in the water. When she realized she was watching the families—the kids—too closely, she gave herself a mental shake and went back to her chair.

Jade and Kase were close, closer than Ledger and Kase. But Jade had moved into her own place over a year before the accident, so no matter how Alys tried to reason through that night, she didn't understand why Jade was with Kase and Zoey. The kids had left the house alone together—Kase and Zoey—and several hours later, Nina Black had called Alys to tell her there had been an accident and she and Fletch should get to the hospital. Nina's son had told her, but to this day, Alys didn't know how he knew. If he had witnessed the wreck. If he had stood by and watched Kase—his best friend—get behind the wheel after drinking too much.

So many questions she would never have the answers to.

That pain was back in her chest, and again, Alys thought about Iva. The way the first time it happened, when Alys thought she was having a heart attack, Iva had calmly talked her through it. Not a heart attack, but a panic attack. She had reminded Alys to take slow, deep breaths. To recognize that the feeling was anxiety, a panic attack, and not a medical emergency. To close her eyes and purposely relax her muscles.

Alys flexed her feet, pointed her toes, and reached for the paperback book she had grabbed from the gift shop when she came down earlier. She didn't do romance anymore, because she couldn't take the happy endings. She didn't read women's fiction, because she couldn't shoulder anyone else's sadness. That left her with thrillers and historical fiction, and she used to enjoy both. It was just hard now to read anything, because her concentration was shot.

Kase and Zoey were leaving to get nachos. And they had planned to go to a party after they ate. A big party at Dandy Camp—as far as Alys knew, the parties had never been too rowdy. The people who owned Dandy were older; their kids had all grown and moved away, but they let local kids gather on the campgrounds and huddle over bonfires and play whiffle ball and badminton. She wasn't naïve. Her kids weren't angels; she hadn't believed that even before the accident. Hadn't she found Ledger and that girl having sex in the backseat of his car when he was seventeen? She knew they drank, but she also knew parents took turns cruising Dandy Camp to make sure things were okay. That no one was out of hand. That there were no brawls or orgies going on.

On the other hand, she knew the kids did fun, innocent things, too, because she'd seen them when she and Fletch had taken their turns at the parental drive-bys. She had seen Jade and Ledger playing badminton with their friends. She'd seen

Ledge by the bonfire, roasting a marshmallow. She'd seen pictures of all her kids and their friends throwing frisbees and even doing silly things like Red Rover.

The police had closed down Dandy Camp, and the owners had moved after the accident. Alys had held her breath, wondering if the Jeffries would sue them for allowing alcohol on the premise, the same way they had threatened Fletch and Alys with a civil suit. Maybe they were somewhat to blame, but every parent whose child went to Dandy Camp knew there would be alcohol there. It seemed a little hypocritical to blow the whistle on something like that after the fact. Alys and Fletch hadn't considered a lawsuit. They knew when Kase and Zoey went to the party that Kase might have a drink.

They had also drilled it into his head to call home if he needed a ride. No questions asked. Just call.

Alys glanced at her cell phone now. Abandoning her book after two sentences, she picked up her phone and scrolled through her contact list, slowing first on Jade's name and then Kase's. She had voicemails saved from both of them, and when she was feeling really low, she played them. Over and over again. She'd memorized them both within two days of their deaths.

Jade's: Hey Mom. Remember that chick I told you about? From work? She got fired. She was totally poaching clients. I told you so! Hey. Wanna do lunch on Saturday? Call me. Where are you anyway? Love you. Bye.

Kase's: Hey. Mom. I'm at the mall. I wanted to grab another pair of those joggers. And I got called in to work tonight. I'll be home in a minute but probably be gone when you get home. I'll grab something to eat when I leave work, k? Love you. Bye.

Her ribs squeezed so hard on her lungs, she couldn't breathe. And when she did manage a quick, shallow breath, it was like her ribs closed harder and tighter, and she could hardly force that breath out. The ache in her chest radiated to her back, and her fingers tingled.

Still, she considered looking at her text messages. She had huge, long text threads going with both Jade and Kase when they were killed. She had never deleted them, though reading through them was like a scourging on her heart, and she didn't do it often.

Before her thumb could betray her and tap the icon, she put her phone down and turned her attention to the pool again. The sun had dipped into the ocean, painting the water in murky purples and pinks. Shade fell over the pool now, and she realized she was cool. The kids in the pool didn't seem to notice the chill in the air.

She opened her book again and forced herself to read.

Where had Fletch gone? Was he with Claire and Josh? A flood of self-hatred engulfed her. Not because of how she had left them, how she had separated herself from them. But because she was hurt that they hadn't included her in whatever they were doing tonight.

SHE WAS ON THE BALCONY WHEN FLETCH RETURNED. Hours had passed; shadows devouring the oceanfront. Alys had changed to her pjs, poured herself two fingers of whiskey, and settled on the balcony, determined to put Fletch and the gang out of her mind. She'd read a few pages of her book, but mostly, she didn't do anything. Or think anything. Or feel anything.

She didn't flinch when she heard the door bang closed. She didn't listen for the sound of Fletch's footsteps crossing the room. But she heard him just the same.

"Hey." He leaned in the open doorway and tipped his head in greeting.

"Hi."

The lamp in the living room behind him put him in a backwards spotlight. Alys catalogued his golf shorts and dri-fit shirt and wondered if he had been out playing again earlier in the day.

"What're you reading?" He tucked his hands in his pockets.

Alys had nearly forgotten the closed book in her lap. She glanced at it and shrugged.

"It's historical fiction, but I couldn't tell you a damned thing about it."

Fletch's grin made her melt just a little. "That's why I just reread old books now."

"You don't like historical fiction?" Maybe she was playing dumb just to keep him talking.

"Because it doesn't matter if I zone out and can't remember what I've read, since I've already read it."

"Mmm." She nodded.

"That and I can't take the twist endings anymore." He shrugged. "Gotta know how it's gonna turn out."

"I hear that," she whispered.

Fletch cleared his throat and took a step out onto the balcony with her. She watched him at the rail, head tipped back and his eyes on the moon.

"Did you eat something?"

He sounded concerned, which she found interesting, considering he took off without a word earlier. But she was too tired to start a fight.

"Yeah. I went down by the pool and had a pasta dish. Drank a glass of wine."

"See anybody you knew?"

"No." She shook her head. "It was kind of..."

The word lonely was on the tip of her tongue, but she managed to stop herself.

"Relaxing?" he suggested.

"Yeah." She nodded and smiled as she looked away. "Definitely relaxing."

"How about you?" she asked after a few minutes had passed.

"Hmm?" He turned to her, hands still in his pockets. "Oh. Went to a dive bar off resort with Claire and Josh."

"Greasy food?" She quirked an eyebrow at him.

"Mmm." He nodded and drew his hand from his pocket to rub his chest. "Feeling it already."

"Do you still take the prescription antacid?"

"I do."

"I have Tums in my bag," she offered.

"I've got some." He lifted a shoulder in a lazy shrug.

Suddenly tired, she yawned and stretched her hands up over her head. Caught Fletch looking at the spot where her pajama top rode up and exposed her belly.

"What time is it?" She ignored the heat in his gaze and her heat under his gaze.

"Almost midnight," he answered. "I'm beat."

"Me, too."

She started to climb up from the lounge chair, but suddenly, Fletch's hand was there offering to pull her up. Alys took a deep breath, but nothing prepared her for the riot of emotion that ripped through her when she put her hand in his and felt his warm skin.

"Thanks," she said quietly. She avoided his eyes and snatched her phone and her book from the table.

"I'll get your glass," he offered, so she hurried inside, desperate to put some space between them. But not even ten minutes later, Fletch crawled into bed beside her. Alys had rushed through brushing her teeth and using the restroom, thinking maybe he would have a drink or take a shower and give her time to fall asleep.

"I thought you might want a break," he said into the dark room. "I mean, you're kind of an island here, stuck with ex-in-laws and an ex-husband."

"No, it's fine," she promised him. "Got some work done this morning. Went shopping this afternoon."

"The burger wasn't done. You would've hated it."

She laughed softly, but she turned her back to him and prayed for courage to get through the rest of the week.

"For the record," he spoke so softly, she had to strain to hear him, "I wish you would have gone with us."

"Fletch." She squeezed her eyes closed.

"I know."

She felt the bed move, like maybe he had shrugged, and then he turned over and mumbled about being divorced.

Alys moved before she could talk herself out of it. She turned to face him and reached for his arm.

"What?"

When he didn't look at her, she scooted closer to him. The press of her breast on the back of his arm got his attention. Still on his side, he rolled his head on his pillow to look at her. Alys cupped his face in her hands and kissed him.

Soft, sweet, and tender.

Everything the sex the other night hadn't been.

"You don't have to feel sorry for me, Allie."

She blinked and let her gaze find his lips.

"I don't, Fletch. I just miss this kind of closeness with another human being."

"Closeness?" His voice was gruff. "You mean intimacy?"

She kissed him again. Nuzzled her nose over his scruffy cheek and kissed the corner of his mouth.

"Goodnight, Fletcher."

Chapter Thirteen

HALLIE LOOKED A LITTLE STRUNG OUT, BUT IT wasn't obvious. No fading bruises. No big neon arrow over her head. No signs of sudden eating disorders or self-mutilation. Alys chalked her outlandish expectations up to living with Iva and hearing tales—no names involved—of her clients' struggles. Still, the dark skin under the girl's eyes was a dead giveaway. Not to mention, she looked to have lost weight she couldn't afford to lose.

When Alys hugged her, she hugged back, but she didn't hang on. Alys hated that; she loved Hallie like a daughter, always had. She held her long enough to feel how slight she was, but when Hallie stepped away from her, Alys was thinking about Ledger. The way he had hugged Claire. Like he was afraid to let go.

How could she love Hallie so deeply, how could she hurt for Hallie, when she let her own son flounder in his grief?

She had dreaded the spa day, but when she was face down on the massage table with her eyes closed and the sounds of

Native American tribal music surrounding her, she surrendered. Her masseuse was an older woman who didn't talk much at all, thankfully, and worked tirelessly to ease every last knot of tension out of her body.

After the massage, she sat in the dimly lit relaxation room, on a lounge chair, with her feet up and a glass of cucumber water at her hand. Brooke and two of her friends were already seated across the room. Alys was so relaxed from the massage, she offered her soon to be daughter-in-law a small wave when their gazes locked.

Next would be a facial. Alys wasn't sure there was a magic wand in all the world that could make her face look young or happy again. But she found herself watching the hallway, anxiously awaiting Claire and Hallie to return. Instead, Julia appeared in the luxurious white spa robe. Dark hair twisted back in a messy bun, she looked shorter and more approachable than Alys had ever seen her.

"That was absolutely incredible," Julia announced quietly as she slowly, gracefully sat on the lounge chair next to Alys. "I have old back injuries from a hiking accident. A professional massage now and then is nice."

Alys offered Julia a smile.

"It was nice," she agreed quietly. Everyone in the relaxation area spoke in hushed tones—it was a rule in the spa—but Alys found it hard to talk to Brooke's mother. She supposed the woman hated her, and she supposed she probably should.

They sat for a moment in comfortable silence, before Julia looked her way again.

"How're you doing with all of this?"

Alys glanced at her, taken aback by her question.

"I can't imagine getting through a day, let alone days like this."

Overcome with emotion, Alys licked her lips and nodded once in response. She took a moment to compose herself, let her gaze wander over the pale blue walls.

"Thank you," she said when she finally trusted her voice. "For asking."

"Step away when you need to, Alys," Julia told her. "I'm so sorry for your loss, too."

Alys cleared her throat and swallowed hard. Would she have brought Iva here? As her guest? Honestly, she would have enjoyed having her here, and Iva would have loved the resort, the coast. Iva had only been to the West Coast once, and that had been a rushed trip. Alys would have liked having Iva here, the one person truly in her corner for this event, but obviously, her ex-husband's family thought she and Iva had been lovers, which would have complicated everything.

Not to mention that she and Fletch wouldn't be rubbing elbows the way they were right now. Who knew? Maybe they would at least return to normal life as friends. Or something a little more than they were.

"Thanks."

She peeked again at Julia, relieved to see the woman had rested her head on the lounger again and closed her eyes.

Iva would have liked the spa day, too. She would have appreciated it much more than Alys. She was low maintenance as far as cosmetics and hair care, but she did indulge in self-care. Massages were a necessity for her.

She had loved deeply more than once when she was younger. Dated and cared for a guy in school, but she told Alys there hadn't been much chemistry between them. Lost a girlfriend to life on the streets and drugs. Iva told Alys she had taken on the responsibility, the guilt, for that, and *she* had ended up in counseling for a while. An only child, Iva lost her parents just after she graduated from college. She'd had friends and colleagues but none to care for her as her cancer progressed. Alys had been grateful for Iva's trust.

Hallie beat Claire to the relaxation room. Alys watched her niece pour a glass of water. Hallie didn't necessarily look like Jade, but of course she reminded Alys of her own daughter. Younger and shorter, darker hair. And yet, she had some of the same mannerisms as Jade, like the way she tilted her head and watched someone talk when she listened.

Alys wanted to scoop the girl up the way she used to when Hallie was four and skinned her knees or when she was thirteen and being bullied in PE class. At the very least, she wanted to hug her again and tell her she would be okay. She didn't, and not just because Alys had no idea if things would be okay—Alys had walked out on her entire life, because nothing felt like it would ever be okay again, so who was she to preach—but because she hadn't seen Hallie in ages, and the last thing Hallie would want is a long-lost aunt gushing over her and making a fuss.

Instead, she took a page from Julia's book and waited until Hallie sat down on her right and simply asked if she was doing okay. Hallie didn't look at her or tilt her head or anything that resembled Jade this time. Eyes on her lap, she answered Alys with a small nod.

It was enough, though, to sit between Julia and Hallie in the quiet room. True, Alys desperately wished Jade was here too.

She even gave herself a minute or two to wonder how Jade and Brooke would get along, if Jade would approve of her for her twin. Hard to say, because Alys hadn't made much of an effort to get to know Brooke.

Once Claire joined them, it was time for their facials. Alys listened absently to Claire and Julia talk, to Brooke and her friends giggling just a few chairs away. With nothing to add to any of the conversations, she was content to listen. Same with the mani pedi time. As much as she had fought the idea the week before, Alys found it very relaxing to let go of all the tension and just be here with the women she was supposed to care about.

Sadly, she didn't feel like a new woman when she headed back to the suite later. Her shoulders, her whole body, felt looser, and she couldn't deny how soft her skin was, and even her French nails were pretty. But she was still dragging her baggage around behind her with every step.

Inside the suite, she stood waiting at the door and listened for Fletch. The rooms were empty. She wondered where he was, but the relief of having the place to herself for a while was overwhelming. Tomorrow the guys were golfing together. Brooke and the bridesmaids were going shopping. Alys wasn't sure what she would do, though most likely, she would end up by the pool again to soak up some fresh air and sunshine.

The day after tomorrow was the luncheon for the ladies, and Thursday was close enough to the weekend to bring official wedding jitters and last-minute things that might need to be done. Alys had no idea what sort of last-minute things might need to be done, because she hadn't been involved in any of the planning. But she was willing to step up and help if anything came up.

A sarcastic snort slipped from her lips. As the mother of the groom, she should *step up and ask* if Brooke or Ledger needed anything. That thought drove her from the entry way to the kitchen, where she splashed a finger of bourbon into a glass. Hating this little kitchen area because it made her think of that kiss she and Fletch had shared the other night and that made her think of that hard, frenzied sex in the entry way and that made her miss the first time they were here when Fletch had laid her out on the bed and worshipped her for hours, she took her bourbon to the balcony off the living room to sit.

Late afternoon sunlight arced off the ocean, sending reflections off the surface of the water. Alys shielded her eyes for a moment and stared at the Pacific, lost in thought. She needed to get up and run again in the morning. She had let a few days go by with little to no exercise. Couple that with the way she was eating and drinking out here, and she would end up packing a few extra pounds home with her. Not to mention what a waste it would be to go home without soaking up as much of the fresh ocean breeze and sunshine as she could.

FLETCH WAS UP AND GONE EARLY AGAIN FOR THE golf outing with the guys. Alys waited until he was gone before getting dressed and heading out to run the trail by the ocean. It was overcast, but even low-hanging clouds over the ocean were something beautiful to look at.

She needed to talk to Ledger. She was his mother, for God's sake. She *wanted* to talk to him. She wanted to know what was going on in his life. But she didn't know how to approach him. Not anymore. He might never forgive her for walking out after losing Jade and Kase, and honestly, Alys wouldn't blame him.

Ledge had been the easier of the twins when they were babies. He had slept better and taken to her breast better, whereas Jade was always colicky and fussy. Fletch had been a dream back then. Never perfect, but damned near that all through the years. Alys had been a fool to leave him, but she would have suffocated staying in their marriage, in that house, with all the loss and the grief.

Alys had loved the twins equally. Always. But you loved differently with each child, didn't you? No less, but differently. Every child needed a different sort of love from both parents. Alys had been free with hugs and kisses when they were little, just as happy to hug them and ruffle their hair and tease with them when they got older. But Jade had struggled a bit in school, when Ledger breezed through everything. Jade went to homecoming as a sophomore, only to have a group of mean junior girls gang up on her the following week at school.

Ledger, though quiet, never seemed to struggle with any of it. Alys didn't have to harp on him about schoolwork. She didn't worry so much about him with his friends.

Would he believe that meant Alys didn't love him as much?

Kase had been the handful. Twice the work as the twins, because he moved twice as fast and got into everything. He had a sharp tongue and had the tendency to talk back more often than not. He was a smartass, but he'd made her laugh every day. She and Fletch had to double down on the parenting with him, doling out more punishments and cracking the whip and making threats over his grades. But that didn't mean she had loved him more than Ledger.

Now she wasn't the mother of three. She didn't have twins. She had one son. A grown man. About to get married and start his own life. And she didn't know him anymore.

Worse than that, she didn't know how to get to know him.

Back in the suite, she grabbed a shower and dressed in loose linen pants and a sleeveless blouse, made coffee, and took her laptop to the balcony to work a bit. More than once, she picked up her phone, thinking about texting Ledge, wondering what she would say. What could she possibly say to explain what she had done? How much damage would it do if she wished him well and walked away again?

She didn't text him, though. No matter what she did or said, now wasn't the time. Ledger was with Fletch today. She had no idea how close they were, if Ledger confided in Fletch, but she wouldn't dream of encroaching on their day.

After reading through email longer than she had planned, Alys closed her laptop and cracked open the book she'd purchased the other day. It took a few pages, and she closed it a time or two to simply gaze out at the ocean and the rocky beach below the resort, but eventually, she lost herself in the story and was stunned to find it was dinner time when she looked up.

Her stomach growled as if to ensure her it was dinner time when she peeked at her phone. She hadn't heard from Fletch all day, so she hoped that meant he was enjoying the time with Ledger. The guys had probably finished their eighteen holes, but she figured they would grab something to eat at the clubhouse grill. No doubt they would have a few drinks. She considered calling Claire to see if she wanted to get something to eat, but she decided against it, assuming Claire and Hallie might like time together.

She was used to being alone since Iva was gone. Even before Iva had passed, she had been sick enough that if Alys wanted to go somewhere to do something, she went alone. Granted, that was rare, but she did get out now and then. Now, she put her book in her purse, grabbed her key and phone, and left the suite.

For an early Tuesday evening, Howie's was busier than she thought it would be. She was relieved, though, not to have to sit at the bar. Instead, the hostess led her to a two-top table on the deck and left her with a menu. She decided on an ahi tuna salad and a glass of Chardonnay, and when she had ordered and was waiting for her food, she took her book from her purse and read more.

Because she was so deeply into the story, she read while she ate. She did look up now and then to survey the crowds around her to make sure no one in her family, no one in the wedding group was here. She was okay alone, but she wouldn't be rude if she were to see anyone she knew. Her gaze swept the horizon now and then, too, watching the sun sink into the ocean inch by inch.

When she was finished, when the waitress took her plate, and brought her another glass of wine, she checked her phone. Her stomach dropped when she saw that the screen was blank. No messages. Surprised to realize she had hoped to hear from Fletch or Claire, she swallowed her disappointment and dropped her phone back in her purse.

It wasn't that she thought the sex the other night, or just the kissing, would patch them back together. But it had crossed her mind since Fletch had shown up and moved into the suite with her that maybe this wedding would at least kindle a friendship between them.

She sipped her wine and read for a while. When she left, she tipped the waitress enough to cover the time she sat at the table to read. The ocean swallowed the last of the sun as she made her way over the resort campus back to the suite. Once there, she kicked her sandals off and dropped her purse on the coffee table.

Two glasses of wine had seemed like plenty at Howie's, but now she wished she had another. If she had one now, she would put her pajamas on and sit on the balcony again with her wine. She used the restroom and then grabbed her book and phone and went to sit outside.

She read until the darkness was too thick to see well, and then she simply closed her book and her eyes and listened to the ocean. When the twins were eleven, and Kase was five, they went to Florida for vacation. They had rented a condo on the beach and stayed for a week. Fletch spent most of the time in the water with Jade and Kase. Alys and Ledger had built several intricate sandcastles. Ledger was never bothered when they eventually washed away or some other kid would step on them or kick them. He simply went to work on another. Kase would get angry and throw a temper tantrum.

Jade and Kase liked to play, tossing a ball with Fletch, or trying to use boogey boards. On the rare occasions they joined family friends on the lake just outside Falls Church, Jade and Kase liked jet skis and tubing. Ledger always preferred a pool setting, where he would swim laps tirelessly, back and forth and back and forth, until Alys worried he would exhaust himself and drown.

Suddenly aware of a low buzzing sound, Alys opened her eyes and grabbed for her phone.

"Hey."

She had expected it to be Fletch, but it was Claire's name on the screen.

"Is Fletch back yet?"

Alys smoothed her fingers over her forehead trying to press a headache away. Smooth away the worry lines that had been chiseled there since motherhood started twenty-five years ago with the pregnancy test that only said positive, not positive times two.

"Um. No." She shook her head and leaned forward to look into the suite. Not like she could see much, but nothing appeared different. She must have dozed off. "Why? What time is it?"

"After ten, Allie." Claire sounded irritated with her. Did she think she was drunk? Maybe that she had passed out?

"I haven't seen him. I grabbed dinner and came back up here. Fell asleep on the balcony."

"Josh got back to the room hours ago. We went back down to the bar, thinking we might find you and Fletch. Josh called him and Ledger, but we can't get a hold of him."

Alys swallowed down the stirrings of worry, but she leaned forward again and swung her legs over the side of her chair.

"You can't get a hold of Ledger, either?"

"Josh talked to Ledge."

"Well, what did he say?" Alys heard the tremor in her voice and wondered if Claire heard it, too.

"Same thing Josh did. Fletch took off after a couple of beers with the guys. No one's talked to him since."

Alys squeezed her eyes closed. "And you're just now calling me about it?"

"Well, I assumed he was fine. That maybe he had a few errands to run or something, but then Ledge told Josh that Fletch kind of flipped out a couple of times on the golf course."

"Flipped out." Alys stood and slipped back inside, worry gripping her belly now like a cold, skeletal hand. "What do you mean?"

"I don't know," Claire insisted. "Ledge just said he seemed on edge. He flipped out. Got angry a few times. Wouldn't talk much. He drank a lot on the course."

"And everybody thought it was okay when he took off? To run errands?" She tossed her book to the couch and ignored it when it fell to the floor. "After having that much to drink?"

Claire's dramatic, frustrated sigh on the other end of the line only made Alys angrier.

"Look, I wasn't there, Allie—"

"Josh couldn't have taken his keys?"

"He didn't realize how much Fletch drank on the course."

Alys paced the length of the living room, chin tucked to her chest and her forehead in her hand.

"Great."

"Will you call me? If you find him, will you call me?"

"Yes. Of course I will."

Alys ended the call, in a hurry to dial Fletcher. Before she did, though, she squinted at her phone to read the time on the screen. It was after ten; she'd most definitely dozed off on the balcony. Wondering if Fletch might have slipped into the suite when she was sleeping, she tiptoed into the bedroom, ready to rail at him and give him hell for scaring all of them.

"Fletch, what the hell—"

She stopped in the doorway and stared at the empty bed. Nothing looked like it had been touched since she had come back from Howie's earlier. Fletch hadn't been here. Her fingers shook with a phantom fear, the memories of the night they lost Jade and Kase rushing at her like a slideshow on fast forward. When the phone started ringing on the other end, she put it to her ear and tried to swallow. Bone dry.

What if—

Jesus, God, what if something had happened to Fletch?

The call went straight to voicemail, which only made her feel worse. She gnawed on her fingernail as she paced the living area again. The sinister shadows in the suite drove her to turn on every lamp in the room. On the fourth floor—the highest in the resort—their suite was probably lit up like a lighthouse from out there on the ocean.

She texted Claire out of sheer desperation, but Claire simply answered that they hadn't found him. On her sixth time across the living room, she swallowed her fear of her son and called him. Voicemail. She considered calling Brooke; her stomach crashed to her feet heavy with frustration when she realized she didn't even have Brooke's number.

What kind of horrible mother didn't even have her son's fiancée's phone number?

What happened with Dad?

She typed out the text, hesitated for a few seconds, and then hit send when the image of Kase's car wrapped around the tree exploded in her head.

I don't know.

The reply came almost immediately, but it didn't satisfy Alys.

What do you mean, you don't know? Did you guys get into it?

Nope. I think he was just thinking about other stuff.

Other stuff? What did that mean? Jade and Kase?

Or Trish?

Alys dialed Fletch's number again.

"Dammit, Fletch, where are you?" she growled when his voicemail picked up again. She eyed the time again—already eleven—and then started to dial Ledger again. The sound of the lock disengaging drew her attention. She looked up as a scowling Fletcher stepped inside and pushed the door closed.

She watched him engage the deadbolt and the chain lock. He didn't appear to be hurt, but his face was set in stone. When he saw her staring at him, he drew in a deep breath and muttered something, stripping his clothes off as he passed by her to go to the bathroom.

He got sun today. Alys took in the red swatch of skin on the back of his neck as he peeled the shirt up and over his head. She used to tease him about golf tans; now she was hungry to look her fill before he disappeared from sight. The sun had turned the skin on his forearms a deep, golden brown, but the hair on his arms was lighter. The thought of what those hands used to do to her made her mouth go dry with longing.

"Fletch?" she called, eyes sliding down over his bare back, his ass in the golf shorts, and his hard, tan calves. He grunted something in response, but Alys stayed frozen where she was and missed it. She heard the pocket door slide closed, and then seconds later, the shower was running.

Still worried, she texted Claire and then Ledger to let them know he had come back to the suite safely.

Chapter Fourteen

CLAIRE CALLED ALYS IMMEDIATELY, BUT ALYS LET her call go to voicemail. She sent another text, explaining that Fletch walked in and went straight to the shower, that she hadn't even talked to him yet. While she was frustrated with Claire for butting in—as if Alys had a claim to Fletch anymore —she was frustrated with Ledger for not checking in further about his dad.

She continued pacing the floor, waiting for Fletch to finish in the bathroom, as if he would just magically appear in the living room with her. As if he would tell her about his day, how the golf outing went, and what he had done when he left the guys.

What had he done? Did he go somewhere to drink alone? Somewhere to call Trish and have true privacy to talk to her?

Claire texted again and then again about ten minutes later, asking for updates, asking to make sure Fletch was okay. Telling Alys to make sure he called Claire if he needed anything, even if he simply wanted to talk. Again, her ex-sister-in-law's horning in on the situation made her angry. She and Fletch might be divorced, but that didn't necessarily mean there was nothing left to resolve between them. Alys and Fletch had lost two children, not Claire and Fletch.

When she realized the shower had been running for nearly an hour, Alys felt that looming dread again. She stopped her pacing and stood at the French doors with her arms crossed over her chest, wondering what to do. Should she check on him? But he was in the shower. Yes, they had been married. Yes, they'd just had angry sex the other night right here in this suite. But that didn't mean Alys would welcome him into the bathroom when she was in the shower or tub.

Still. It wasn't like Fletch to do this. First to just disappear like he did. And now to linger in a shower, behind closed doors for this long. If Alys needed the restroom, she could use the half bath just off the foyer of the suite. Technically, it shouldn't matter to her at all if he came out of the bathroom all night. It did, though.

She tiptoed to the pocket door and stood for a moment to listen to the shower water splatter on the floor. There was no movement. The splatter sound was steady, like the water was just sluicing over his still body continually. Had he passed out? Was he drunk when he came in? She hadn't thought so, but if he had been drinking all day and night, he couldn't be sober. Alys hadn't gotten close enough to him to smell any alcohol on his breath.

She rested her hand on the door and took a deep breath.

Still nothing.

"Fletch?"

No answer, of course, because she spoke quietly, cautiously. She had to check on him. For one thing, if she didn't, she wouldn't put it past her sister-in-law to come charging into the room with the bellhop, claiming it was her room or that the man staying in the suite had been murdered by his ex-wife.

"Fletch?" she asked again. This time she knocked. When there was no answer, she slid the door open partway, intending to just peek in and make sure he was still on his feet in the huge, marble shower. Through the steam billowing in the room, she could see the glass shower door. The steady spray from the showerhead, falling straight to the marble floor. No Fletcher.

"Fletch?" she called as she slid the door all the way open. "Fletch, you okay?"

There was still no answer, but now she could see his toes. His leg stretched out over the floor, shower water beading on him and sliding off. Her heart slammed into her throat. What the hell was going on? Had he passed out? Was he sick? Maybe he had been weird on the golf course because he wasn't feeling well.

Her heart skipped up her throat and into her mouth, and she gasped as she took a step into the bathroom. Her shaver was in there.

What if—

He wouldn't.

Fletch was a strong man. Physically and emotionally strong. They had suffered through a horrible loss, but they had come out on the other side, and life might never be happy again, but they would survive.

Except she had left him.

Alone.

Assuming Claire and Josh could pick up his pieces and put him back together while she was off somewhere alone, gluing her own broken pieces back together.

"Fletch?" she whispered as she walked further into the room. Again, she knew he didn't hear her say his name. But when she stood even with the shower, she groaned with relief. No blood. Just Fletch sitting with his back to the shower wall. Apparently, he heard her groan, saw her sway on her feet. As Alys reached for the gold handle on the shower door, he squeezed his eyes closed and tapped his head on the wall hard enough to hurt.

"Fletcher?" She pulled the door open, heart hammering in her chest now.

"Go away, Allie," he said softly. "Just go away."

"Are you okay?"

He answered her whisper with his own groan of pain. The sound broke, and she realized he was crying.

"Fletch. Oh God, baby, what's wrong?" She kicked off her shoes and walked into the shower.

"Don't." He rolled his head on the wall and finally met her eyes. "Just go. Leave me alone."

"Talk to me." She squatted beside him, her right side already soaked with his cold shower water. "Talk to me."

"Why?"

The word was almost a bellow, but his lazy shrug took the sting out of it.

"Why would I talk to you? Now?"

"Fletch." Slowly, she eased herself to her knees and reached for his hand. Her fingers brushed his cold, clammy thigh, but as she picked up his hand, he lifted it to push her away. "What happened?"

"Lost my kids in a fatal car accident and then, for fun, my wife divorced me."

His sarcasm cut her, but she didn't flinch.

"You've been drinking."

Alys winced at his sharp stare. She twisted around to sit on her butt and pulled his hand to her lips.

"Did you and Ledger get into it?"

"No." Fletch bent his knees and tugged his hand away from her to rest his elbows on his knees. "It just gets to me sometimes."

"Jade and Kase?" She wrapped her fingers around his forearm and squeezed gently.

"I'm out there having a good time with my son. With Ledger. And Josh and Roark. It's all great, and then we're on the seventh hole, and Ledger shanks his drive. He was so pissed. I knew from how he swung his club around after he teed off that he wanted to throw it. He was thinking about throwing it. And it just—it hit me."

"That's the way Kase was," she whispered. "Hot headed."

Fletch nodded. He dropped his head to his hands and rubbed his forehead, pushed his fingers up into his hair.

"I got stuck on that day he got in a fight with the kid next door. When he went after him with a bat."

Alys bit her lip. Seven-year-old Kase had been pissed at the neighbor boy for breaking his wiffle ball. To this day, Alys still figured it was an accident. Didn't take much to dent a wiffle ball. But it didn't take much to piss Kase off, either. Kase chased the kid around with the plastic bat for a good minute before Fletch caught him mid-swing. Fletch took the bat off his upper arm. Alys had flinched, knowing it had to sting. But her husband had calmly taken the bat from Kase, took Kase by the arm, and marched him into his bedroom where he got a talking-to and a time out.

"And the day his boss gave him hell at work for slacking on the job," Fletcher continued. "Third damned day stocking shelves at the hardware store, and he was slacking. Just like Kase."

Alys held her breath for a second. She slid her hand up his arm and tugged, but he wouldn't budge. With her back to the water now, her wet linen slacks touched Fletch's bare leg. The water spattering on her back was icy; she wondered how long ago it had gone cold.

"Babe," she started, intending to at least talk him out of the shower.

"Fuck you, Alys." He still mumbled, but this time he lifted his chin and boldly met her eyes. She wondered if the red lines in his eyes were from alcohol or if he had been crying that long.

"Fletch, I'm sorry." She scooted closer, pressing her leg hard against his and leaning her upper body into his. "I'm sorry."

"You fucking killed me when you left." He swallowed and then huffed out a harsh breath. "Like I didn't know it was my fault. That you would blame me. I still didn't think you would—"

"Wait. Wait." She shook her head and scooted closer still. "Fletch, I didn't blame you. I don't blame you."

"Right." He nodded, his voice thick with sarcasm again.

"How was anything that happened your fault?"

"I should have protected them. Right? I was their father. I should have protected them. I should have done something to stop Kase from drinking like he did. I should have taken his keys away—"

"You weren't there," she whispered. "Fletch, we weren't there. It was an accident."

"My beautiful baby girl." He clenched his teeth and ducked his head again. "Just gone. Just." He shrugged. "Gone. Daddies always protect their girls. And I didn't. And you left."

"Fletch."

Desperate to console him, Alys moved back to her knees and ignored the pain of the tile floor on her joints.

"I didn't leave you because I blamed you," she whispered. Fletch didn't react until she wrapped her arms around him and pulled him against her. His clammy skin stuck to her silk blouse. Alys smoothed her hand back over his wet hair, cupping the back of his neck and drawing him closer to kiss his head. "I didn't blame you."

"She squeezed my fingers, Allie," he gushed as he turned into her and grabbed her hard and tight against him. "In the hospital, she squeezed my fingers. I kept talking to her, begging her to hold on. I thought..."

She hadn't known that. Fletch had never told her Jade had reacted to any stimuli in the ER. They had rushed in and grabbed at their children before a team of doctors and nurses rushed them away and then let them die.

Not fair. Alys flinched and then sucked in a deep breath as tears slid over her cheeks. The doctors and nurses had done absolutely everything they could to save them, but Kase had died in the ambulance, and Jade was gone within minutes of arrival.

Sometimes, like lancing a boil, it relieved the hurt just a bit to blame someone else.

But never Fletcher.

"Oh, Fletch—" Her throat wouldn't work anymore. The knife in her chest had moved to her throat, and Fletch's fingers dug into her back so hard it hurt. But she couldn't move. Even if she wanted to.

"I'm sorry, Allie," he said now. "Sorry...my fault."

"It's not your fault."

His fingers moved up her back and twisted in the wet fringe of her hair until she pulled back to look at him. Up close, she saw the raw desperation in his eyes, probably the same look she had given him the other night in the foyer.

But when he kissed her, she was disappointed in the lack of pain. She needed him to bite her, to sink his teeth into her lip or to snap at her tongue. She needed to hurt more with him here and now than she hurt in her head and heart.

"No." He shook his head when she dragged her hand around his face and framed his mouth with heavy fingers. "No. Not like that."

"I just need it to hurt," she confessed.

"I can't, Allie. I can't hurt you. I need to heal you."

He loosened the tight hold on her hair and dragged gentle fingers over her shoulder and up her neck to trace her cheekbones, his mouth still pressing sweet, tender kisses to hers. Alys parted her lips to breathe, thrilling when Fletch did the same. His lips hovered near hers for a moment, and finally, he nuzzled her mouth with his, only to kiss a trail over her chin and down her neck. Could he feel her pulse on his lips?

Fletch dotted kisses over her neck again, and this time, he leaned in and flicked her earlobe with his tongue, and finally, finally, he was back at her mouth, ready to take. To drink her in. His hands were still feather soft on her face and her neck. His lips moved persuasively rather than possessively. Alys kissed him back, breathless when he pulled away from her.

"Why?" His low, gruff voice broke on the word. Before she could make sense of his question, he flicked her upper lip with his tongue and then delved deep between her lips to stroke hers.

Iva had kissed her like this once. She had been insanely curious one night after too much wine. The kisses had led to other things that left Alys feeling both shamed and guilty.

"Why did you leave me?"

Another long, sensual kiss stopped her from answering. Drove Iva out of her mind. Alys lost herself in the taste of beer on his breath, on his lips. She slid her tongue over his and over his teeth, hungry for the way it used to be between them.

"If you didn't blame me, why did you leave?" Fletch drew away from her, abruptly ending the kiss. Alys struggled to catch her breath, surprised at the heat between her legs when she was sitting in cold water. She met Fletch's eyes, the intimacy in the kissing, the position they were in, the things they had done to each other's bodies like exposed electric wires in the water with them.

"Fletcher." She closed her eyes, unable to take more of the charge, the spark between them. Still panting a bit, she pressed her fingers to her lips and shook her head.

"You could at least give me that much, Allie."

"I couldn't handle your grief…" The words ripped out of her in a wail. "On top of mine."

"What?" He pulled at her hand. His touch made her open her eyes.

"I was drowning, Fletch. God, the hurt was so bad, and it never stopped. It just never stopped. I felt like someone had ripped my fucking heart out, and I would never stop bleeding. I couldn't handle that and you. And Ledger."

"I never saw you grieve."

"Nice," she muttered with a slight nod.

"No." He squeezed her hand when she tried to pull away. "No, I'm not being a dick, Alys. I just…you were so collected. So cold. I wanted that same barrier around me, to protect me. I didn't know how to do it. How you did it. I just wanted something to turn the pain off."

She sniffled and wiped at her eyes.

"We need to get out of here," she announced. "The resort's probably out of water, and Claire's probably out there knocking the damned door down."

Pain shot up through her knees when she rocked back to her heels. Her clothes were heavy and cold on her skin. She almost welcomed the misery. When she stood, she reached for Fletch's hand again, breathing a small sigh of relief when he took it and climbed up from the floor.

"How long has the water been cold?" she asked him when he leaned around her to shut it off.

"Not that long," he mumbled.

As cold as he was, she found it hard to believe. But then, when she had come into the bathroom, steam had billowed through the room, so maybe he was telling the truth. Fletch pushed the shower door open, and Alys stepped out. She grabbed the towel he had placed on the bar and handed it to him, watching when he scrubbed it over his hair and then down over his arms and shoulders. She warned herself to stop, to look away, but she couldn't. When Fletch buried his face in the thick towel, she let her eyes roam over the hard plane of his chest, down the v of his abdomen, and over his penis, impressive even now after sitting in the cold water.

"Why would Claire be knocking the door down?" he asked when he lifted his head. Alys felt a rush of heat in her cheeks when he caught her looking at him.

"She called me earlier. Worried sick about you, because no one knew where you were."

"Christ," he muttered. "I'm an adult."

"Who took off after drinking too much," she reminded him. "Did you drive?"

"I'm not irresponsible, Alys," he said with a sigh as he dried off his upper body. She shivered uncontrollably, her clothes still plastered and dripping from her body. "I took an Uber."

"Good." She nodded.

She reached for a towel, but she hesitated when she felt him watching her.

"Allie."

"Fletch, I can't."

"Just let me see you."

It might have been the desperation in his voice, or maybe it was the look in his eyes, but she waited a moment and finally nodded. She put the towel down again on the edge of the tub and slowly began to peel her clothes off. It didn't feel sexy, letting the soaked clothing fall to the floor and standing nude before her ex-husband. She felt raw, exposed, and the longer he looked, the more she wanted to cover herself.

Goosebumps climbed her arms and legs, and her nipples beaded hard and tight with the cold air on her wet skin. She watched Fletch knot his own towel around his waist, but she ducked her head and looked away when he leaned around her to get her towel. Rather than hand it to her, he rubbed it gently over her shoulders and down her arms.

The tender touch was her undoing.

She stepped back and shook her head.

"No."

"I can't get it up right now, anyway, Allie." His voice was almost distant, like he was lost in his own thoughts. Maybe he was, because she was certainly thinking of other times.

"Fletcher." She hissed when he trailed his fingers over her bare breast, pausing to tweak her nipple, before he went back to drying her off. On his knees before her, he rubbed the towel over her thighs, down the back of her calves, and over her feet.

"You never minded whiskey dick before."

"Fletch." She breathed his name as he whisked the towel back up over her knees to her thighs.

"Let me touch you?"

Their eyes met. Alys parted her legs the slightest bit and dug her teeth into her lip when he eased his hand between her thighs. Liquid heat pooled there, his nearness making her blood thick and heavy as it moved through her body.

She wanted him. She wanted to reach down and spread herself wide for him, to feel his breath there on her skin. He dropped the towel on the floor, abandoning the ruse, and molded his hands up the backs of her thighs.

"Fletcher." Her mouth was dry, but she was wet for him, ready for him when he leaned into her and pressed his open mouth to the spot where her panty line would be.

A sudden sharp, loud ring tore through the suite. Fletcher jerked back and looked up at her with a frown.

"What the hell?"

"It's the doorbell," she reminded him.

"Room service?"

The peel of noise sounding again grated on her nerves, pressed on her shoulders, and pierced through the back of her neck.

"It's your sister."

"Dammit." He rested his head on her belly. Alys stared at his neck, at that vulnerable soft skin, and still struggling to catch her breath, she pressed her fingers to the back of his head. Claire wasn't likely to give up, but Allie's body vibrated with the need to finish what they had started. When they were married, when Fletch drank too much and couldn't get it up for her, he ravished her body with his mouth.

"Just touch me," she whispered. The memories of the way he used to lick her and suck her to make her orgasm made her shiver right now, and her eyes burned with tears. "Fletch, just one touch. It won't take much."

He kissed her belly and then nibbled his way to her hip. Alys rocked up on her toes when he slipped his hand between her thighs again and pressed his thumb to her core. Her soft moan turned into a long, deep guttural cry when he drove his fingers up inside her and found the spot that rendered her completely helpless.

The doorbell pierced the quiet again, and then the only sounds were Fletch murmuring something over her hips and the delta of curls between her legs and her gasping to breathe and chanting his name.

"You okay?" he asked, the top of his head pressed to her belly again.

"Yeah."

"I'll get Claire," he offered as he slowly climbed to his feet.

She nodded, grateful for a minute to herself. Fletch rolled the pocket door closed as he stepped out of the bathroom. Alys looked at herself in the mirror, amazed at the flush in her face. The orgasm had breathed life into her; she didn't recognize the woman in the mirror.

Chapter Fifteen

SHE WOKE ALONE THE NEXT MORNING, WHICH wasn't necessarily a surprise. For one thing, Fletch had been up earlier than she was most mornings they had been here. For another, she wasn't sure what to think of what had happened between them last night, so she figured he had no idea, either. Not to mention, he had dressed quickly and gone out to talk to Claire last night, and Alys had taken some time alone to brush her teeth and put dry panties on with her pajamas and gone on to bed.

What bothered her when she finally sat up in bed was the fact that his side didn't appear slept in. She shoved her hair back from her face and looked at the nightstand, hoping for coffee. Disappointment sank her belly. She grabbed her phone thinking maybe he had at least texted her, but there was nothing from Fletch. Just four missed calls and a texted command from Claire.

Call me.

No. She couldn't deal with Claire right now.

She slipped out of bed, her thoughts on how well Fletch knew her, how he had played her body to make her come so quickly last night. True, she had been ready to orgasm just with his nearness and thinking about the things he used to do to her. But still, Fletch had always been generous and confident in bed, and he knew his way around her body.

At the French door in the bedroom, she pulled the curtain back and studied the ocean for a moment. Their marriage hadn't been perfect, but it had been close enough. *Fletch* had never been perfect, and she knew he would say the same of her. But they had celebrated twenty-five years of marriage before everything fell apart.

If only she could turn back time.

She padded to the bathroom to take care of business, determined not to get caught up in the memory of the night before. Finding a broken Fletch in the shower. Reacquainting herself with the lines and muscles in his body. His shoulders. The ropy veins in his forearms. His solid thighs. The v she used to kiss while her breasts rubbed gently over his penis.

Her cheeks were pink again when she washed her hands. Not from embarrassment. She and Fletch were too old to be embarrassed about the things they had done together. Sex was a natural thing between two people attracted to each other. They had been married for a lifetime, and they had created children together. There was nothing wrong about what they had done together.

No, her cheeks were pink again with desire. Arousal. If he were here right now, she would lead him back to bed and straddle him.

The pillow and folded blanket on the couch stopped her in her tracks. Fletch had slept on the couch. The sofa that was much too small to accommodate his big male body. The sofa that was nowhere near as comfortable as the bed they had been sharing without complications for several nights now.

Now her face flooded with embarrassed heat. She had ventured into the shower to talk to him, to save him, not seduce him. And yet, somehow, they had ended up naked together, and Alys had all but begged him for the release.

And rather than sleep beside her after that intimate moment, he had chosen to sleep on the couch. Never mind that they had been married for a lifetime, they were divorced, and Fletch had moved on.

She swallowed hard, the knot in her throat painful. She could play that game, too. In fact, she had been the one to start the game, and by God, she wouldn't quit now. On knees weak with rage and hurt, she moved through the living area to the kitchen to brew her own coffee. She barely had the ground coffee in the basket and water in the pot when the damned doorbell rang again.

"Who in their right minds thinks a hotel suite needs a doorbell?" she grumbled as she made her way through the dining area to the foyer. It would be Claire. No doubt, she was going to open the door and find her sister-in-law there, most likely mad and mean about yesterday.

"What?" Alys yanked the door open wide, not giving a damn that she was still in pajamas.

Claire stared at her boldly. "Could you have just called me back?"

Alys huffed and stepped aside. She tossed her hand up as an invitation to come inside. Unfortunately, Claire accepted the invitation and hurried in before Alys could change her mind.

Claire followed her to the kitchen and propped herself in the doorway. As bold and unapologetic as she had been not even ten minutes ago about being intimate with Fletch last night, her hands trembled now under Claire's heavy stare.

"What do you want?" Her voice was gruff. She poured the water into the reservoir and then slid the pot on the burner before turning to Claire.

"Why didn't you call?"

"Did you not come here after midnight last night and ring that damned doorbell three times? Didn't you talk to Fletch?"

Claire shrugged. "I did. But I wanted to talk to you."

"Why?" Alys tossed her hands up helplessly.

"To make sure he's okay."

"You talked to him, Claire."

"Did you?"

Alys jerked her gaze away from Claire, but she nodded.

"What did he say? What happened?"

"What did he tell you?"

"Just that sometimes the grief is overwhelming, and he needs to step away and be alone."

Alys shrugged, but she jerked her head up and down in affirmation.

"Yep."

"Alys."

"You interrupted us last night, Claire," she snapped, finally meeting her ex-sister-in-law's eyes again. "Okay? Are you happy? He was on his knees in front of me when you rang the damned doorbell."

"You guys are having sex?"

"No," Alys answered immediately, but the other night in the foyer flashed in her mind and she shrugged, her shoulders heavy with guilt. "Sort of."

"Well, this is great." Claire sighed and rubbed her forehead.

"I'm sorry?"

"Don't mess with his head, Alys," Claire pleaded. "He was a basket case after you left. He's—"

"So much so that he found another woman before the sheets got cold, Claire. Remember that?"

"He needed someone to lean on."

"He had you."

"He needed more than I could give him."

"And what? I just didn't need anything?"

"You walked out," Claire reminded her. When the coffee maker beeped, Alys was relieved to turn her back to the woman and pour herself a cup.

"Do you want some?"

"No."

She sipped and flinched when the scalding hot liquid filled her mouth and burned down her throat.

"Look, I thought when I told you he had come in safely last night that would be good enough. You came here after midnight and interrupted something, and you talked to

Fletch, so you know he's okay. So why are you badgering me now?"

"Because I don't know he's okay," Claire said simply. "And now, knowing your gonna mindfuck him all over again, I'm even more worried."

"What happens between us is our business. Not yours."

"Do you know he went on a five-day bender when you left?"

"Do you know how many times I considered suicide before I left?" Alys tipped her head. The shock on Claire's face made Alys' heart and belly drop. She regretted the words immediately. Not necessarily because she had upset her ex-sister-in-law, but because she felt like she had just sliced her heart open for Claire's scrutiny.

Claire's mouth worked, moved arounds words she apparently couldn't find her voice to speak. Alys flicked her gaze over Claire's face, but she looked away quickly when she saw the tears in her eyes.

"Suicide?" Claire whispered. "You thought about killing yourself?"

Alys sniffled and stared at her hands now wrapped around her mug. "I couldn't deal with it. I couldn't drag myself out of bed. I couldn't even open my goddamned eyes, Claire. If I kept my eyes closed, I could pretend. I could pretend it was all a nightmare."

"Allie." Claire sighed.

Alys flinched when Claire put her purse and phone on the counter.

"Don't." She shook her head. "I don't wanna talk."

"You need to talk," Claire insisted. "You need to talk. You have never just let someone be there for you."

"I can't!" Alys snapped. "I can't do it." She put the mug down and watched coffee slosh over the rim to the counter.

"Do you talk to Fletch?"

"No." She shook her head.

"Iva?"

"Please go?" She turned her back to Claire and hunched her shoulders in an attempt to disappear.

"Dammit, Allie, I love you. Let me help—"

"I have to go to lunch today with my son's fiancée. I have to pretend that I still have a heart. I have to pretend that anything in the fucking world matters to me. I have to find a smile for Brooke and her girlfriends and her mother." Alys turned to Claire, teeth clenched with desperate rage. "I can't do this right now. I cannot do this, Claire."

Claire stared at her silently for a torturously long moment. Afraid she was going to ask again or worse, offer advice, Alys turned back to the counter. She licked her lips as tears rolled over her cheeks. She had shared her thoughts with Iva. All the ways she wanted to kill herself. Iva had calmly countered with all the reasons she shouldn't.

That and insisted she talk to a doctor about medication.

"Okay." Claire cleared her throat. "Okay. I'll go. And I'll see you at lunch."

Alys nodded and pulled away when Claire pressed her fingers to her arm. She tensed when Claire picked her stuff up and headed out of the kitchen. When she heard the door open and close, Alys collapsed against the counter and sobbed.

THE WALK DOWN TO FURY FOR LUNCH WITH THE girls was both interminably long and far too short. Every step she took left her feeling more and more vulnerable, walking alone through the hallways and the crowded lobby, but every step took her closer to an afternoon event with a group of women she had no desire to be around.

She wished she could make Claire understand it was nothing personal. Alys wanted, needed, to be left alone. With her next step, she wished Claire was by her side to give her a little strength as she walked into the restaurant.

Fury was fancier than she would have liked, but she couldn't blame Brooke for that. Every woman deserved to be treated like a princess for her wedding, and Brooke was no exception. Truthfully, Alys approved of Ledger's fiancée. If she liked people these days, she would like Brooke.

The sleeveless silk sheath dress had never been uncomfortable before, but at the moment, Alys was miserable. The arm holes felt tight, as if the material was cutting her armpits. The waist felt tight, even though the dress barely hugged her slender hips. The coral silk fell to her knees, so it was appropriate, but today it felt ridiculously short. Her small wedge heeled sandals rubbed her toes. By the end of the day, she would have blisters.

Except probably not. Because she would most likely be stuck at this luncheon all afternoon.

"You look gorgeous."

Alys jumped and looked to her left as Claire fell into step beside her. Embarrassed now by the breakdown earlier, she refused to meet her eyes and looked away quickly.

"Love the color."

"Stop it."

They walked a few more steps before Claire looped her arm around Alys'.

"No. I'm not gonna stop."

With their arms entwined, Alys felt her shrug.

"I had gifts shipped out here," Alys mumbled. She swept her gaze around the resort campus. Several small white tents on the northern lawn caught her eye. It was too early for the tents to be for Ledger and Brooke, but they might be for someone else's wedding. "I hope they arrived."

"I did, too."

"Where's Hallie?"

"She actually spent last night with Brooke and her friends. She came in for a shower earlier and took off again."

"Wow." Alys quirked an eyebrow at Claire. "That seems like a good thing."

"Yeah, I think so."

Thinking about Hallie reminded her of Jade. Of the fact that Fletch thought she had left him because she blamed him for not protecting their babies. Thinking about Fletch made her think of her low, throaty moan last night when he put his fingers inside her to make her come.

Which reminded her that he had chosen not to sleep next to her. Last night of all nights. They had had sex a few nights ago, but it was last night that he chose not to sleep by her. Last night had been too intimate. Too slow. Too tender. Alys had wanted his touch, not his cock to drive out her demons.

"Where'd you go?" Claire nudged her side with her elbow, but Alys only shook her head.

She hadn't lingered in the shower earlier for obvious reasons, but she had taken care with her hair and makeup. No need to show up at her future daughter-in-law's bridal shower luncheon looking like a zombie. Inside Fury, a few tables were taken, and there appeared to be more than one group of women there to celebrate with a future bride. Alys took it all in—the stiletto heels and the dresses and makeup—relieved that she had forced herself back together at least for today.

When Alys couldn't find her voice at the hostess' stand, Claire told the woman they were there for the Reynolds-Holland wedding shower.

"Follow me," the woman chirped, and before Alys could give in to the dread weighing her down, threatening to paralyze her, Claire gave her arm a gentle tug. Obediently, Alys fell into step with her, and they followed the hostess to a long table in the back of the room. The double glass doors were open to the ocean, and the sound of the waves crashing was the perfect backdrop for conversation. Alys felt herself relax just a bit. The ocean did that to her.

"Alys!" Brooke noticed her first. Claire gave Alys' arm a gentle squeeze as Brooke approached them. "Hi. I'm so glad you're here."

"I'm happy to be here," she said quietly. It was suddenly true, but she couldn't infuse any joy into her voice. Not if she wanted to sound sincere. "You look beautiful, Brooke."

The girl blushed a bit. She nibbled on her full lower lip and then reached awkwardly with her left hand to hug her. Alys stepped closer and put her arms around her.

"Thank you," Brooke whispered. "I know this isn't your thing, but it means a lot to me that you're here."

"I wouldn't miss it, sweetheart." The words slipped out without her okay. Words she might have said to Jade back in the day. And again, though soft-spoken, they could not have been more honest.

When Brooke stepped away from Alys, she greeted Claire warmly. Alys felt the hard jab of jealousy again, followed immediately by guilt because she had been the one to cause the rift in the family. Rather than listen to Claire and Brooke talk and dwell on how green it made her feel, Alys drifted away and spoke to Julia.

"Hello." Julia offered her a bright smile and began introducing her to Brooke's friends. Hallie gave her a sweet smile, and then everyone moved at once to sit down. Alys found herself on Brooke's left, while Julia was on her right. She wondered if Brooke wouldn't prefer to sit with her girlfriends, but she supposed the kids had been going out nightly and this was a proper event that dictated Brooke do the polite thing.

Claire settled on Alys' left. They ordered drinks and lunch, and little by little, Alys felt the knot in her belly unwind. Of course, the wine helped. But so did Claire, though she was loathe to admit it.

She found her voice and crushed the anxiety, the weight of grief, under some unknown strength, and participated in conversations about the wedding plans. When lunch was over and Brooke opened her shower gifts, Alys sat attentively and watched her. She smiled and nodded in the right places. Sipped her wine. Fell into an interesting conversation with Brooke's matron-of-honor. The girl was a technical writer for a documentary series, and Fletch had always been interested in documentaries, so naturally, Alys was pulled into conversation.

When Brooke opened Alys' gift, it took Alys by surprise. While she had picked out the Waterford crystal toasting flutes, she had left them at the service counter at the jewelry store to be gift-wrapped and shipped to the Kahalina Bluffs Resort. She didn't recognize the paper, so her words in Brooke's voice startled her.

Wishing both of you the world, together. Love, Alys.

Brooke dabbed at her eyes and peeked at Alys. She whispered a thank you, and maybe to the rest of the women at the table, Alys appeared cold. Drowning now in memories of the day she purchased the flutes, she couldn't swallow. For just those few moments that day, she had absolutely loved Ledger and Brooke and honestly wished them everything good life could offer.

And then she went home and stared down the bottle of prescription antidepressants that Iva had insisted she take. It had taken every ounce of willpower she had to put the cap back on the bottle and walk away.

Suicidal thoughts just a few months ago. Alys wasn't sure they would ever go away.

Chapter Sixteen

THE LUNCHEON STRETCHED THROUGH THE afternoon, as Alys suspected it would. Once Brooke finished opening her gifts and her matron-of-honor listed each gift and who it was from—a job Alys wondered if Jade might have done had she been there—Claire ordered another round of cocktails. Alys wondered about Fletch, where he was. What he was doing. While Claire didn't appear to be worried for his physical safety today, Alys was preoccupied with what Fletch might be thinking.

The shower became a pool party, and Alys was swept along with the rest of the girls and women, caught up in the excitement and yet still separate from it. She considered playing hooky the rest of the afternoon, once she was back at the suite to change from her dress to her swimsuit. But Claire texted to make sure she was coming, and Alys had no doubt that if she didn't show up at the pool, Claire would march over to the suite and hunt her down.

It felt good to lounge by the pool. Obviously, it was more relaxing, though Alys still would have preferred to be alone. By dinner time, anyone not in the wedding party and or part of the wedding guest list had fled the pool area, and the music had changed to top 40s. Alys declined Claire's invitation to sit with her on the side of the pool, content to relax on a deck chair with a glass of chardonnay at hand.

Eventually, the guys joined them, and Alys' ideal afternoon was shattered. She found Ledger first, watched him for a few moments, and wondered if he was happy. Not with Brooke; it was obvious to Alys they were made for each other, and she wasn't around them much at all. No, she wondered if Ledger was happy in general. If he was satisfied with his current life, his career choice, and the future he and Brooke had mapped out together. If Brooke completed him or if there was still a gaping hole inside him that belonged to his twin. If he missed his little brother.

They started a rowdy game of volleyball in the pool. Oddly enough, it didn't bother Alys, although she figured it was probably good that there were no other guests on the pool deck now. Claire attempted to stay on the side of the pool to watch the game, but Josh scooped her up and dropped her in the water. The amused snort that slipped from Alys' mouth startled her, but no one else seemed to have noticed. No one called out to Alys for her to join them.

Mostly, she was okay with that.

But she might have liked it if Fletch had asked her to play. Or even looked her way. Apparently, he was more upset about what they had done the night before than she had assumed. It hurt a little that he was freezing her out, as if he thought she might read the situation wrong and make assumptions about the rest of their stay.

"Hey."

Alys rested her head on the chair and looked up at Brooke.

"Hey. Why aren't you playing volleyball?"

Brooke, glass in hand, shrugged dramatically and looked at the chair next to Alys.

"Can I join you?"

"Sure."

Alys watched Brooke drop to the chair like a ton of bricks. Her future daughter-in-law took a drink and then fell back against the chair and closed her eyes.

"You okay?"

"I'm exhausted," Brooke admitted. The corner of her mouth tipped up, and she peeked at Alys through hooded eyes.

"Oh, kiddo, this ain't nothing." Alys laughed softly. "You're gonna be dead on your feet by the time your wedding rolls around."

Brooke grinned. "Ledge and I are gonna sleep through the honeymoon."

"Oh, I doubt that." Alys rolled her eyes. "I'm not sure Fletch and I ever closed our eyes on our honeymoon."

"Yeah?" Brooke tipped her head and studied Alys' face. "Seriously? Like you did it with your eyes open?"

"Don't you?" Alys quirked an eyebrow at her. "All the better to see everything."

Brooke snorted and covered her mouth.

"I think Ledge better cut you off."

Brooke closed her eyes and rolled her head back and forth on the chair. "Nope. It's water."

"Water?"

"Mm-hmm."

A collective shout went up from the pool, followed by a loud wave of laughter. Alys glanced that way, watched her son hop out of the water to chase the ball down.

"Let me guess." She looked back at Brooke. "Worried about the dress fitting come Saturday?"

Brooke's smirk flatlined, and she took a moment to study the glass in her hand.

"You really don't have any idea what's going on, do you?"

"Going on with what?" Dread twisted Alys' body apart; her heart climbed into her throat, and her belly dropped hard enough to hurt.

"I'm pregnant, Alys."

As if Brooke realized she was about to repeat the word, only loud enough for everyone in the pool to hear her, she sat forward and lunged at her. Paralyzed with shock, Alys watched Brooke's fingers curl around her wrist, her perfectly manicured nails overlapping. Mouth agape, she looked from her hand to Brooke's eyes and then glanced at the pool.

"You didn't know."

"No. I didn't."

"When was the last time you talked to your son?"

Alys stirred and snatched her arm away from Brooke's grasp.

She fumbled around for something to say, but before she could utter a word, Brooke cut her off.

"Seven months," she told her.

"Seven months what?"

"Since you talked to Ledger. And he called you. He left you a message, but when you didn't return his call, he called you again. Remember that?"

She did remember that. She was driving, leaving the cemetery. Even when Iva died, it was easier to talk to her than grieve for her own children. Sad and exhausted, she had taken Ledger's call. Infused some fake energy into her voice, though she knew to Ledge she sounded fake and uninterested.

"Yes."

"Do you remember what he said?"

"You were working. He was fixing dinner. And you guys were planning to go to your friend's daughter's dance recital."

Brooke gave her a slight nod. "Yeah. And did he ask if he could come and see you?"

Alys blinked and looked away. He hadn't outright asked her if he could visit, but he had kind of meandered through some words that sounded like a half-ass offer to get coffee or lunch.

"He mentioned getting coffee."

"Mmm. And you told him no."

"I had meetings the rest of that week." Alys ducked her head and pinched the bridge of her nose.

"You blew him off."

"I didn't blow him off," she snapped. "He suggested getting coffee, and I couldn't."

"How many times since you left him and Fletcher has Ledger called and suggested getting coffee?"

Alys took a deep breath. She understood the point Brooke was trying to make. Something big had happened if Ledger had actually reached out to her, and rather than be his mother and listen to him, she blew him off because she was too busy to care.

That wasn't it, but she couldn't sit here and explain that to Brooke. She wasn't about to dive into her own misery, the way she had been drowning at home with the weight of Fletch and Ledge's arms around her neck.

"We called the wedding off," Brooke announced.

"What?" Alys sat forward and swung her legs over the side of the chair. "When? Why?"

"Well, the first time I gave him the ring back was about a month after he proposed. And then about seven months ago."

"What are you talking about, Brooke? What happened?" She chanced a glance over her shoulder, relieved to see the volleyball game going in full force.

"He needed you," Brooke whispered. "He won't admit it, but he still does."

Alys flinched when her stomach lurched. She pressed her hand to her belly and tipped her head at Ledger's fiancée.

"Brooke? What happened?"

"He's emotionally unavailable at least ninety percent of the time." Brooke shrugged.

"You love him." She needed it to be true, so Alys didn't phrase it as a question.

"Oh, I love him so much, it hurts," Brooke agreed. "Doesn't change that he can be a coldhearted jerk sometimes."

"And that's my fault?"

Brooke turned to look at Alys and rolled her eyes.

"Why did you call off the wedding?" Alys ignored the look. Of course, it was her fault if Ledger was emotionally unavailable. Although, she wanted to defend herself, to argue that Ledger was the least emotionally excitable of her children.

"The first time we got in a huge fight," Brooke said simply. "About the wedding itself, actually. I wanted a big church wedding. You know, trumpets and a long aisle for me and my dad. And, like, everyone blowing bubbles as Ledge and I hurried outside to a waiting convertible that would drive us off into the sunset."

"And?"

"Ledge wanted to go to the justice of the peace."

"Fletch tried that when we got married," Alys mumbled. "That's hardly reason to call off a wedding."

"He didn't want to invite family. He didn't want to ask you to be here. He wasn't sure he wanted to tell you we were getting married at all. And he wasn't sure he wanted Fletcher at the wedding."

The words tore a hole right through her middle. Alys fixed her gaze on Brooke and refused to give in to the pain.

"Yeah, even then, I could have let it go, right? No big deal. We'll get married with just my family and our friends there.

But." Brooke raised her brows and shook her head. "I pushed it. Because it felt like a huge red flag that he wanted to start our life together by avoiding you, avoiding his family. Avoiding the grief none of you have processed. Loving Ledger is one thing, but I wasn't ready to walk into marriage with him, knowing that when shit got hard, he ducked his head in the sand to hide."

"Like I did," Alys said quietly. "Right?"

Brooke met her eyes without apology. "Yes."

"But you worked it out?"

Brooke rested her head on the chair again. Her chest puffed up on a deep breath; Alys watched her cheeks puff up, too, and then Brooke shrugged as she let the breath out.

"Yeah?" She licked her lips. "It's not that I don't want to be with him. I don't want to lose him. Ever. But I want him to find some peace with all of this. To forgive himself. Me loving him isn't enough to make him happy. He needs to find that in himself."

Alys rested her elbows on her knees and covered her face with her hands.

"What happened the second time?"

"I had a miscarriage." Brooke spoke quietly, but the words were loud and harsh, and they rang in Alys' ears and her bones and her heart.

"What?"

"I got pregnant before Christmas. It wasn't planned, but we were so excited." Brooke shot Alys a quick peek. "We started making plans. Looking at baby stuff. Planning her room—"

"Her?" Alys' voice broke.

"Ledge wanted a baby girl," Brooke whispered. "We didn't know. I wasn't that far along."

Alys dipped her head again, and behind the protection of her hands, she pulled in a long, slow breath.

"Picked out names." Brooke sniffled. Alys held herself still, praying Brooke didn't say Jade, because that name right now would shatter her beyond repair. "Felicity. We were gonna name a girl Felicity."

Alys breathed a bit easier, though her chest ached.

"For happiness." Brooke's voice hitched this time. "Felicity Jade."

Alys blinked and swiped at her eyes.

"For a boy?"

"Daniel Kase." Brooke's answer smothered Alys. She looked up and gasped for air, but the fiercely protective look on the girl's face kept her butt firmly on the chair. "Do you know what the name Daniel means?"

She mouthed the word no.

"'God is my judge.'"

Alys waited for Brooke to continue.

"I chose the first names, Alys, because I desperately need to see him happy. And I need him to remember no one judges him. No one. But God. Not me. Not Fletch. Not you."

Alys lifted a trembling hand to push her hair back from her face.

"And not himself."

"I don't judge him." Alys shook her head. "I've never judged him about anything."

"Ledge thinks you do."

"What?"

"Ledger believes the accident was his fault, and he believes down deep in his bones that you blame him for what happened."

Alys flinched. She climbed to her feet and took a step away from Brooke, from the pool. She dabbed at her eyes, her stomach again ready to revolt, her throat choked with emotion.

"It wasn't his fault," she whispered.

Brooke climbed to her feet and followed Alys back behind the chairs. In the shadows of the cabanas, Alys thought they might be hidden from sight. All the better for Brooke to finish the attack, drive the knife in deeper. Nothing could hurt more than what she had already said.

"I know that." Brooke shrugged.

"Why does—why does Ledge think I blame him?"

"Because you left!" Brooke shouted. Beyond caring if anyone could hear them, Alys didn't even bother to look over her shoulder. "You left him. You lost Jade and Kase. And you walked out. And you stopped loving your other son. The one that survives."

"That's not true."

"No?" Brooke tipped her head. "Really? You sure as hell have a funny way of showing you love someone."

"I don't know what happened that night, Brooke, but I have never blamed Ledger. Ever."

"Kase called him that night," Brooke announced. She read Alys' surprise on her face and notched her chin a bit like she had scored a point. "He needed help. Something had happened with him and Zoey."

"Do you know what? What happened?" Alys asked begrudgingly.

"Why? Is that more important?"

"No." Alys clenched her teeth together, afraid she would explode any moment.

"Zoey popped some pills. Kase had no idea she did it, and when he found out, no one could tell him what it was. He called Ledge and begged him to come to the party to help him. Kase had been drinking. Zoey passed out. She hit her head when she fell. Ledge was talking to me that night. We had been together for a few months at that time—"

"I didn't know that."

Brooke arched her eyebrows as if to say no kidding.

"I was on break. It was a hell of a night. I just needed him. To talk. I needed his voice. So, when Kase started texting him and then calling him, he got pissed. Told Kase to fuck off."

Alys flinched.

"So, Kase called Jade. They were taking Zoey to the ER when Kase lost control. Jade had texted that much to Ledger before the accident."

Alys crossed her arms over her belly, shoulders hunched to protect herself from more verbal blows.

"Why didn't he just tell me that?"

Brooke snorted. "Really? Because he blamed himself. If he had gone, he would have died instead of Jade. And then at least you might have lost Kase, but you would still have Jade."

Alys shook her head before Brooke could continue.

"No."

"The miscarriage broke us up," Brooke whispered. "He was out with friends when it happened. Golfing. I waited too long to call him. Thought I would be fine. He blamed himself."

"Do you blame him? For the miscarriage?"

"Of course not." Brooke shrugged. "Jesus, Alys, I'm a nurse. At least ten percent of known pregnancies end in miscarriage."

"But you called off the wedding."

"He shut me out. He chose to wallow in his guilt rather than supporting me. Grieving with me. Loving me."

Alys' nostrils flared with her deep breath. She wasn't stupid; whether it was Brooke's intent or not, she saw the parallel between herself and her son. Damned if she would acknowledge it out loud, though.

"How did you fix it?" Her whispered words were almost lost in the sounds of the fun and games in the pool.

"I gave him the ring back," Brooke said simply. "And I told him I wouldn't marry him until he figured out how to deal with his emotions. With all the baggage he was still dragging around from the accident. With the miscarriage. With my need for him to be more open. It's hard to make love when you get a cold shoulder in every other room in the house."

Alys licked her lips and eyed the fencing around the pool deck. She supposed it was hard to make love when a relationship had no intimacy. She'd done that to Fletcher. She'd shut down on him, and yet, she had begged him for hard, rough sex when they were alone. Because she needed to hurt more on the outside than she did on the inside.

"And did he? Figure it out?"

"He went to counseling," Brooke mumbled, but she shrugged dismissively. "But really, it was more that we were still seeing each other. That even when it hurt, we were together. That even when we made eye contact, we were both thinking about our Felicity or our Daniel, we still found the smallest thing that we could smile about. Laugh about."

Alys sighed and nodded. Probably, talking this out with his mother might have helped Ledger.

"I mean, it sucks." Brooke nodded, her eyes bright with tears. "And I'm in no way suggesting that losing my baby when I did is comparable to your loss, Alys."

Alys gave her a curt nod, but she said nothing.

"Ledger had to figure out that it's okay," Brooke whispered.

"That what's okay?"

"It's okay to be happy again. It doesn't mean he loves Jade or Kase any less. Doesn't mean he and I won't always remember our first baby."

Brooke reached for Alys' hand, but she let her own fall to her side before touching her.

"It's okay to be happy."

Chapter Seventeen

SHE WASN'T IN THE MOOD TO MINGLE, SO WHEN THE pool gate closed behind her, she didn't look back. There was no way she could look at her son right now; knowing what she had done to him made her sick. Trying to talk to Ledger on a good day was difficult. Talking to him now? After Brooke dumped all their struggles at her feet, with an audience of family and friends? Alys wouldn't last ten seconds before she lost control of her emotions.

Still angry, a little bit hurt after Fletch blew her off all day, she fantasized about grabbing a handful of his hair and yanking him around to look at her. To listen to her give him hell for what happened, for not sleeping beside her after sliding his fingers inside her and drawing out that incredibly intense orgasm, for not checking in with her at all today. She wouldn't give him the satisfaction. Odds were, he and Trish had rocked the walls in her apartment, and that few minutes alone the night before with Fletch's fingers inside her and his breath on her hip bone meant nothing to him.

She didn't want to retreat to the suite, either. The thought of being there alone, knowing that they were all still at the pool having a good time stole her breath away. The fact that she had chosen to separate herself from her family notwithstanding, she nursed hurt feelings as she wandered away from the pool. Rather than entering the resort, she walked the path from the pool around to the front of the resort. The sun had slipped low enough in the sky to throw shadows beyond the main resort building. Alys slowed her steps to admire the flowerbeds, cast a glance at the parking area past the cottages, and wished for just a moment that she could hop in the rental and drive. And never come back.

Running away hadn't solved anything the first time, though. In fact, she had only made things worse. For Fletch and Ledger. And for herself. For the first time, she wondered what she would do, how she would feel, if Fletcher married someone else. If he married Trish.

If he had children with Trish.

Would those babies replace Jade and Kase?

She dismissed that last thought instantly. Even if she could have more children, she wouldn't. She had no desire to do it again, and no one would ever take Jade or Kase's places in her heart. Why would Fletch feel any differently than she did?

But he could still remarry.

Alys huffed out a frustrated sigh, because the idea of Fletcher married to anyone else, loving anyone else, being happy with anyone else, made her sick, even angry. She didn't want him. She didn't want him to be with her, did she?

But if she didn't, did that mean she only wanted him to be as miserable as she was? Forever? Was she really that small of a person? Had grief stripped her down to a knot of mean, hateful feelings forever aimed at the only man she had ever loved?

She wouldn't run again. She couldn't now, anyway. Her keys, her purse—everything was back in the suite. Even if it was her plan, being back there now, after being there with Fletch again —talking to him, fucking him the other night, moaning with pleasure at his touch last night—she wouldn't make it one step outside the suite. She had tied herself to him again, for better or worse, but even more than that, she owed it to Ledger to stay here and watch him marry the love of his life.

And talk to him.

Alys wandered inside the lobby, pausing just past the doors to take it all in. Kahalina was such a beautiful place; it felt sacrilegious to be preoccupied with envy and heartache. Hunching her shoulders to the chill of the air-conditioning, Alys crossed the marble floor and headed to the bar. Never mind that she was in a swimsuit; the simple black cover up looked like a dress. She needed something stiff, and since Fletch had ghosted her all day, she had to settle for a drink.

Rather than the jazz music she and Fletch had listened to the other night, a guy she figured was supposed to look effortlessly put together but, in all reality, had probably primped and fretted over the white linen pants and button-up powder blue shirt and the slicked back blond hair played easy-listening music if the current song was any indication. Alys chose a seat at the bar, ordered a shot of bourbon, and tried in vain to block out the James Taylor song. Listening to "Don't Let Me Be Lonely Tonight" was akin to rubbing salt in her wounds.

Brooke had shocked her with the things she said. Alys' skin still prickled, trying to absorb the pain, the hurt Brooke had projected at her. She was angry, ready to tear into the girl and tell her she had walked away from her son and her husband, because she couldn't ever forgive herself for the loss. Because she could never allow herself to be happy again. Because she couldn't give them comfort when the loss had stripped her down to the bone and left her a vicious, raging pile of venom.

But she understood, too. In fact, as she sipped the bourbon, Alys realized she was a tiny bit thankful Brooke had slapped her in the face with the hard truth. Not because Alys had the guts to do a damned thing to fix it. But because Brooke had shown her true colors, and Alys had no doubt that she was the only woman for her son.

Transfixed with an imperfection in the black granite bar, Alys rubbed her thumb over it and wondered if Ledger had talked to Claire. When Alys blew him off, had he gone to Claire? Would Brooke have told her? Or would she even know?

What would come of Alys when this weekend was over, and they all went back to their lives? She had severed all these ties, and now she was practically living in her ex-husband's pocket, joined at the hip with her ex-sister-in-law. But when the wedding was over, they would go home, and Alys would be alone again in Iva's house.

What would Iva think about the intimate moment with Fletch? She might be jealous, but she would also say something like I told you so. Alys pushed that thought away, uncomfortable thinking about the few intimate moments she had with Iva and the way Iva insisted she was still in love with Fletch.

Next to her, a couple argued about spending money on a new boat. Alys cupped her fingers around the glass tumbler, determined not to throw it back and ask for another. She fisted the fingers of her other hand and rested her forehead on her fist. Eyes closed, she listened to the wife nag the husband about the ridiculous amount he had paid for the boat. The husband seemed indifferent to the nagging, which roused Alys' anger just a bit. Until he spoke and mentioned someone named Tad. That if he needed an out while she was fucking Tad, so be it. Maybe her anger on the wife's behalf was misplaced.

Alys used to be a good listener. Empathetic. Giving. Tender. When her babies were small, she cried when they did. Their growing pains were hers. She championed her friends, her family, rallied the troops when times were bad. She loved without condition, and it was that deeply rooted love that had driven her away from Fletch and Ledger. Taking on their pain, on top of her own, on top of her guilt, was suffocating her.

And dying there in her marriage, in her family, would only have hurt them more.

Hours later, she made her way back through the lobby to the suite. She had nursed the two fingers for the duration of her bar time. Heard two more arguments between lovers. Heard heated whispers between other lovers. And ignored more sappy love songs.

It was only ten when she closed the door behind her. Her phone remained quiet, so she had no idea where Fletch was. Pretending she didn't care, she moved silently through the living area to the bedroom where she undressed. Silence ticked around her as she washed her face and brushed her teeth. For a moment, she gave in and met her own eyes in the mirror.

As if she hadn't scrubbed hard enough, Brooke's abrasive words still painted her face. Everyone assumed she had left for selfish reasons, and maybe that was better. She would grit her teeth and get through this weekend. And then she would go home. To the house Iva had left her. And she would do her penance for hurting those she loved.

Alone.

In her late-forties, Alys assumed she had several more years of life ahead of her. She could torture herself with images of suicide, of the feeling of cool, calm relief, but she would never give in. That would be her easy way out, and she had to punish herself.

Still alone, she slipped her pajamas on and padded back to bed to slip in between the cool sheets. Iva had touched her once. They had kissed passionately, and wine had made her a little happy and dizzy, and Iva had trailed kisses over her breasts and touched the throbbing wet heat between her legs. The orgasm had seemed particularly potent, but then, it had been months by then since she and Fletch had been together.

When Alys rolled away from her, overcome with shame, Iva had kissed her shoulder, rubbed her arm, and promised it was okay. Iva might have wanted Alys to love her, but she had only ever been giving. Never demanding anything in return.

Alys was awake when Fletch came in. She lay on her side facing the wall and listened to him move through the suite. A tiny piece of her withered and burned when she heard the French door open and close. She pictured him on the balcony, the wind in his hair and his eyes on the ocean. She could join him, but he had made it clear he didn't want her company.

She peeked at her phone, surprised it wasn't even eleven. Alone with your thoughts in the dark was the scariest place to be, and she felt as if she had been lying there alone for hours. Her thumb hovered over the message icon, but she had no one to talk to. Nothing to say. Instead, she tossed the phone back on the nightstand and waited, wondering which would come first—Fletch or sleep.

She might have dozed off, but she heard him when he went to the bathroom. Flat on her back, eyes open, she listened to the sounds of his nightly rituals. The shower, quick this time, and brushing his teeth. When the door slid open, the steam rolled out, bringing with it Fletch's signature scent and so many memories, Alys ached inside.

Watching him tiptoe into the bedroom in his snug boxer briefs, she wondered if he planned to sleep on the couch. Housekeeping had cleaned and the bedding on the couch had been removed, but that didn't mean he wouldn't sneak out there again.

"What're you doing?" she asked when he reached for his pillow.

"Giving you space." Worse than angry, he sounded defeated. A little bit dead inside.

She could let him go, but she was suddenly terrified of spending another hour alone in the king-sized bed.

"I never asked you for space." She propped herself up on her elbow and reached for his hand.

His irritated sigh cut through her like a steel blade. Embarrassed now, she dropped her hand to the bed and nodded.

"You didn't want me here," he reminded her, wrapping his hand around his neck and squeezing. "Remember that?"

"Aren't we passed that now?"

"Fucking you in the foyer the other night was one thing," he hedged. He met her eyes briefly, long enough that she saw the pained look on his face. "Last night was a little much."

Her soft, sarcastic laugh escaped before she could catch it.

"Right." She nodded. "Of course it was."

"Allie, I don't know what you want from me."

She considered telling him to go to hell. Suggesting that he spend the rest of their time together on the sofa. But she didn't want to. She wanted his solid presence beside her. She needed him there in the bed with her more than she needed her next breath.

"I don't either, Fletch."

His guttural groan suggested pain. Agony, even. He gave her his back and dropped to sit on the edge of the bed.

"You were my everything." His voice sounded like gravel and glass and sand and heartache. "You and I lost our babies, and then I lost you, and you were everything in my life. You were my life."

He leaned to rest his elbows on his knees and hung his head.

"I loved you so goddamned much."

"Fletch." His name stuck in her throat and came out thick and mangled.

"I finally learned how to breathe again, and then last night happened, and I..."

"You what?" She sat up, the sheets sliding to her waist.

"I wanna throw myself in the fucking ocean, because when this weekend is over, odds are I'll never hear from you again."

"That's not true," she argued, but her voice was too soft, too weak to sound honest.

"I was hard for you all day," he continued. "And it wasn't just my dick that wanted you. It was my mouth. My hands. My lungs...I just want to breathe you in and consume you."

"Fletch." Cautiously, she shifted toward him.

"My heart, Allie. My heart is gone for you."

She pressed her palm to his back, startling at the heat in his skin. The jolt of longing that scurried up her arm straight to her nipples. Afraid but desperate, she moved to her knees and inched closer to him.

"It hurt," she whispered over his skin as she pressed her lips to his shoulder.

"When I touched you?"

"Realizing you spent the night on the sofa. Rather than sleep with me."

He scrubbed his hands back over his head and groaned again.

"I thought..."

"You thought what?" He looked at her over his shoulder, his bloodshot eyes narrowed suspiciously.

"That you would...at least...text me. Call me."

"Is that what you want?" he asked. "Because I figured you would be angry. With me for pushing you. With yourself for letting your guard down."

"I was angry," she admitted.

"And now you're angry with me for trying to do the right thing."

Alys smoothed her fingers over Fletch's arm, stroking the hard muscle under his hot skin. He muttered something when she drew away from him, but it didn't stop her.

"I was angry with Claire," she told him as she pulled her pajama top over her head and tossed it aside. "For interrupting us."

Flames smoldered in his eyes as he turned to her. Alys felt his gaze as he took in her nude breasts, her heart hammering with fear when he didn't reach for her.

"Please don't say no."

"I can't fuck you." He shook his head. "I won't."

"Fletcher." She flopped back to sit on her butt, humiliation heating her face now. "I need you."

"Fucking never fixed it before." He shook his head. "I can't treat you like a whore, Allie. Hurting you makes me sick—"

"I need you to make love to me." She lifted her eyes to his. "The way you used to."

His hand shook as he reached to cup her chin.

"Where did you go? When you left the pool?"

"Took a walk."

"What did she say to you?"

"Fletch, please."

He stood and turned toward the bed as he shoved the briefs over his hips and his cock sprung free. Alys eyed him with greed and reached for him as he slipped into bed beside her.

Chapter Eighteen

SHE CRIED, HATING TO LET GO OF HIM TO DASH AT her eyes as he moved inside her. Ridiculous to want to hide the tears from him, and yet, she dreaded the moment he would notice them. His hands were tender, and he smoothed her thighs and her belly with gentle strokes, as if he took pleasure in molding her back together. His kisses were slow and sweet and long and deep, drawing more tears and shivers and soft moans from her lips.

She turned her head to offer her neck when he inched backwards over her and parted her legs to bring him home when he nestled there between her thighs. His lips tugged at her nipples; his tongue tracing the curves of her breasts. Alys hooked her foot behind his thigh to bring him closer, grabbing his face to kiss him when he lifted his head to look at her.

As good as it was to take, to lie back and let Fletch love her, it wasn't quite enough. Weight on her elbow, she slipped her arm around his shoulder and cupped the back of his head in her hand. She nipped at the bow of his lips and dipped her tongue inside his mouth, led by hunger and greed. Once there, though, she slowed, drawn to the care, the love, Fletch wanted to give her.

Sex with him the other night, angry and hard, her back slamming into the wall over and over, had been just what she needed. At that moment. Now, in the dark of night, with the waves of the ocean crashing gently outside the balcony door, with the mattress at her back and Fletch's warmth, his strength pressed against her, wrapped around her, she gave in to that crushing ache inside. Breaking the kiss, she nuzzled her nose over the scruff on his cheek and down to his neck. Once there, she rested her head on his shoulder and squeezed her eyes closed and let him love her.

Rather than drive into her, he eased inside her cautiously, as if letting her body remember him, remember his girth, his length, the feel of him filling her. He found her lips again and kissed her, tasting the salt of her tears as she couldn't hold them in anymore.

Tonight, she didn't want it to end, and as if he could read her mind the way he used to, Fletch was slow and thorough. Arms wrapped around his shoulders, his neck, she held on and followed his lead, reaching for heaven, falling short each time he pulled back to tease her. When she was breathless and wrung out from the climbs and the falls, she sank her nails into his shoulders and begged, pleaded for him to make her fly.

When he did, she sobbed his name out loud, and when he held her as she soared through the stars, her skin tingling and her body quivering with pleasure and pain she had almost forgotten, she chanted his name like a prayer, her lips and her teeth on his earlobe, as if she could swallow him whole.

"You okay?" His voice was tight and sharp, his body hard like stone above her. Heat radiated from his skin, his heart pounded against her breast pressed against him.

"Yes."

"Can I come? Inside you?" He brushed his lips over her cheekbone and met her eyes, waiting for her permission to do what they had done hundreds and hundreds of times before.

"Yes."

She shifted beneath him and squeezed him as he moved over her again, his motions harder, his hips jerking and pounding with his need to be deep inside her. The rutting sounds he made as he pumped harder and faster still sent a thrill of power through her, and then he froze over her, his head high, his neck exposed to her, and she sank her teeth into him as he hissed with male pleasure and satisfaction.

This is when she would have said she loved him.

But because she did, because she loved him desperately, she clenched her teeth and let the aftershocks of her orgasm roll over her and bowl her down, content to drown in Fletcher.

THEY AWOKE STILL TANGLED TOGETHER AFTER A night of lovemaking. They slept nude with the sheets off and then on, and Fletch woke her once to slide into her from behind her and made sweet love to her while she kept her eyes closed. Alys woke once to find herself wrapped around Fletcher's back, as if to clothe him. In the light of morning, she woke to him spooned behind her again, his right arm around her, his hand cupping her breast.

"You okay?" His voice at her ear was gruff with sleep.

"Stop asking me that."

"I have to ask, because the first time you aren't, I have to let you go."

"I'm okay." She nodded, her head still on her pillow.

"You might be sore today." He pressed a hot kiss under her ear and fiddled with her nipple.

She laughed softly and covered his hand with hers. "Might be worth it."

"Might?"

She grinned when he leaned way over to see her face.

"You were four for five," she mumbled with a shrug.

"I could go for five out of six," he suggested.

She rolled over to her back and met his eyes.

"No. I can't do that. Not in the daylight."

"I kissed you to orgasm in the garage at noon on a Saturday while the kids were out riding their bikes."

She grinned. "That was before."

Fletch flopped over to lie on his back, pulling her with him. She tucked herself under his arm and rested her head and hand on his chest.

"Claire's gonna be pissed."

"Because I didn't get you there that one time?"

Alys laughed softly. "Because we had sex."

"We made love, Allie," he corrected her.

"Worse yet, in Claire's eyes."

"I'm not worried about my sister," he promised her. "Besides, the only way she'll know is if you tell her."

"Does Trish like it?"

"Like what?"

"Oral sex."

Fletch pursed his lips and sighed. He lifted his head a bit to meet her eyes and studied her with a frown.

"Are you asking me if I could make her come that way?"

"I am."

"Sometimes."

"It's weird," Alys admitted.

"What is?"

"Picturing you with your face between someone else's legs."

"Tell me about it."

"What does that mean?" She traced the outline of his pecs and dragged her hand down his hard stomach.

"It's not exactly easy picturing someone else with his or her face between your legs."

"Never happened."

"I saw you kissing her once."

"I did." She shrugged. "But..."

"You were living with her, Allie. You're wearing her ring. Last night when we made love. Even now, you're wearing her ring."

"It's a ring that meant something to her. To her family. There was no one else for her to give it to, Fletch. That doesn't mean we were having sex."

Fletch stroked his fingers down her arm. "Really?"

"No. We messed around a few times. Things got a little out of hand once—"

"What does that mean?"

"She touched me."

"She made you come."

Alys nodded. "Yeah."

"With her fingers?"

"We had been drinking. I knew she was attracted to me. We talked about it. I was curious. The kissing turned me on. One thing led to another."

"What was it like?"

"It wasn't you." Probably not what he was asking, but it was the only thing she could say. As much as she cared for Iva, she had never replaced Fletch in her heart.

"Did you touch her?"

"Not like that."

When he didn't say more, Alys dipped her head to press her lips to his chest. She nudged his nipple with her tongue.

"Does it bother you?"

"Hell yes, it bothers me."

"That I was with a woman?"

"That you were with anyone," he answered. "You were supposed to be mine."

"Do you know Ledge and Brooke are pregnant?"

"What?"

"She's pregnant," Alys whispered.

"Is that a good thing?"

"I hope so."

"Then we should celebrate."

Alys laughed as Fletch hauled her up and tugged her over to straddle him.

"I don't think celebrating our first grandchild with sex is appropriate." She covered his hands with hers when he cupped her breasts.

"We're not gonna do that," he promised.

"What are we doing?"

He moved his hands to the backs of her thighs and tugged her closer.

"I'm gonna feast right here," he told her as he lifted his head and pressed his open mouth to her core.

THEY ORDERED ROOM SERVICE AND HAD COFFEE AND breakfast in bed. After a shower, they dressed and headed out for a drive in Fletcher's rental car. Alys needed time to process what they had done, the things he had said. She needed to be alone; she needed that space now, but she was terrified to ask for it. While she couldn't take him back, while she refused to chase their past for happiness, she didn't want to hurt him. Not again.

They drove the Pacific Coast Highway, the radio tuned to classic rock. Alys had worried that the intimacy through the night, even this morning when he had driven her to the edge with his tongue and then pushed her over to freefall with his fingers and his teeth, that he would expect her to talk. To confess her undying love for him. That he would expect everything to be different. Better.

She wasn't sure she would ever be ready for things to be better.

Because nothing would ever be better for Jade and Kase.

He didn't push her, though. He didn't ask for assurances. He didn't make her promises she wasn't ready to hear. He drove. She watched the ocean out the window. They stopped for lunch at a bistro an hour north of the resort, and even then, they sipped a glass of wine and shared a plate of shrimp and fries. Took in their surroundings. But they didn't talk. Not about the night they shared.

"Brooke told you she's pregnant?"

"She did." Alys nodded.

Fletch linked his fingers with hers as they walked back to the car.

"Hmm."

"I thought you wanted grandchildren."

"I wanted to have grandchildren with you," he said simply.

"Fletch, they lost a baby last winter."

Fletcher stopped walking. His nostrils flared as he drew in a deep breath. "Poor kid can't catch a break."

Alys folded her arms over her chest. "I know." She nodded. "But I love how she loves him."

He stared at her for a long moment. "Good."

"When you..." She hesitated and looked at him over the hood of the car.

"What?"

"When you told me you didn't love her..."

The only indication that he heard her was a quirk of his eyebrow.

"Were you lying to protect my feelings?"

"Do you think I could make love to you the way I did last night and love another woman?"

Guilt stabbed at her, poked her in the heart and her belly, spreading hot pain through her fingers.

"Did you love Iva?"

"Not the way I loved you."

She wasn't sure she meant to say it that way, past tense. She wanted to call the word *loved* back, but it was too late. Fletch visibly shrunk before her eyes, flinching at her word choice.

"We should get back." He glanced at the watch on his wrist. "The rehearsal will be starting soon."

Shame and sadness like a brick in her belly, Alys nodded and climbed into the passenger seat, the easy silence of before now heavy with regret.

THEY DIDN'T SPEAK EVEN AFTER FLETCH HANDED the keys to the valet and ushered her through the lobby. Sorrow crawled through Alys like a worm as they wound their way back to the suite, the deserted resort hallways offering no relief from the awkward silence that grew with each step.

"You can get ready first." Fletch's offer broke the silence as they neared the final turn in the corridor. Alys cleared her throat, but when she found she still couldn't find her voice, she simply nodded.

Brooke was waiting at the door of the suite. She glanced over her shoulder as they approached, her face frozen in a mask of fear. Alys swallowed hard, her stomach twisting with worry for Ledger.

"Hey, Brooke."

"Fletcher." Brooke's lips stretched in a bloodless smile, but she immediately looked back at Alys.

"Is something wrong?" Surprised to sound normal, Alys took a deep breath and offered up a silent prayer that Ledger was okay. Never mind that she hadn't believed in God since he had taken Jade and Kase.

"No." Brooke shook her head with a frown. "I um...I was just hoping I could talk to you for a second."

Alys bit her lip to keep from reacting. More? Brooke had more to say to her?

"Of course." Her calm voice belied the storm in her belly.

Fletch tapped the key card to the lock, pushed the door open, and waited for the two of them to enter before following them.

"I'll go get ready," Fletch offered. "Give you two some space."

"Thanks." Alys nodded, but she really wanted to beg him to stay. To stand beside her and hold her up. She folded her arms over her chest as she watched him retreat and disappear into the bedroom. Alone now with her soon to be daughter-in-law, Alys drew a deep breath and gave Brooke her full attention. "What's going on?"

Brooke fidgeted for a moment and then as if she was as flustered as Alys but determined to get through the next few minutes in one piece, she dropped her hands to her sides and steeled herself with her own deep breath.

"I owe you an apology."

Not at all what she was expecting, Alys simply stared at her.

"I was out of line last night. The things I said to you." Brooke avoided Alys' eyes as she stumbled her way through her apology.

"No, you weren't."

"Your grief...is off-limits. I can't possibly imagine what it's like for you, and I had no right to judge you."

Alys side stepped her and moseyed across the living room to the balcony, leaving Brooke to follow her if she chose.

"Did Ledger get angry with you? For talking to me?"

"He doesn't know I said a word," Brooke spoke directly behind her.

Alys rested her hands on the railing and watched the waves lap at the huge rocks on the beach.

"You can't imagine my grief, and I hope to God you never have to." She licked her lips. "But that doesn't mean you were wrong to confront me."

"I didn't mean any disrespect." Brooke edged up to stand beside her. "I just want Ledge to let go of his guilt. I need him to be happy."

Alys glanced at her and closed her yes.

"It's hard," Alys turned to face Brooke, "to have those ugly truths thrown in your face, and maybe I was angry last night. Maybe I was hurt."

"Alys—"

Alys shook her head quickly to stop her.

"But you had every right to call me out on how I've treated my son." She sniffled and dabbed at her eyes. "You have every right to love him so fiercely."

"I do," Brooke whispered.

"So protectively."

"I just wish..." Brooke ducked her head and hesitated. When she looked up, tears streaked her cheeks. "I know he loves me, Alys. But I know there's still a deep, dark sliver inside him full of hatred and fear, and maybe it's selfish of me, but I want all of him. I want all of him to love me. And our baby."

And Ledger needed Alys if he was ever going to be the man Brooke needed and deserved.

"I know." Alys gave her a curt nod.

When she didn't say more, Brooke huffed out a sigh and wiped at her eyes.

"I should probably get going," she mumbled.

"You should. Go find some happy, Brooke. This is the time of your life."

Brooke took a step toward the door.

"You'll be there, right? Tonight?"

"Of course we will." Alys pushed her hair off her face and then swiped at her eyes again.

"I just...when I knocked earlier, and you didn't answer..." Brooke bit her lip and met Alys' eyes briefly. "I thought..."

"I promise you. Fletch and I will be right there with you and Ledge tonight and all day tomorrow."

She wanted to promise more, but she couldn't.

"Thank you." Brooke nodded and rushed inside. Alys turned back to the ocean and waited until she heard Fletch emerge from the bathroom before going inside to get ready for the evening.

Chapter Nineteen

ALYS AND FLETCH WALKED DOWN TO THE WEDDING rehearsal together, though neither of them had much to say. To his credit, Fletch did ask if everything was okay with Ledger and Brooke, but when Alys said yes, he let it go. Alys wasn't sure how she felt about that; she wanted to talk. To dig into the heartache, the tumultuous feelings twisting and spinning through her belly, her blood. She wanted Fletch to be curious, to be concerned. She needed him to push now, the way Brooke had last night.

But it wasn't the time. If ever they were to dig into that pit in her belly, it would be ugly, and Alys would be feral in her grief. There had been tears since Jade and Kase had been gone, but she had been so rigid, so controlling as to never collapse in front of anyone else. Compassion in the face of her rage, her despair, would be her undoing.

The sunset painted the sky in an array of pinks and oranges, and the white vinyl folding chairs the staff had arranged for the wedding were half in shadow and half in the evening sun. A shaft of sunlight fell over Ledger and Brooke as they stood in front of a white trellis, bejeweled with calla lilies and white roses. Ledge looked so handsome in the khaki-colored trousers and navy button-down shirt. Tomorrow, of course, he would wear a suit, and it struck Alys that she hadn't seen him in a suit since the funerals.

Greedy for signs of happiness, of friendship and love, Alys watched Ledge with Brooke as the wedding planner moved a bridesmaid here or there and reminded an usher of this duty or that. Ledge and Brooke stood facing each other, fingers linked, sharing whispers and laughter. Alys used to know her son well enough to read his emotions on his face. Now, though, maybe she had taught him how to rage, to hate, behind a poker face.

The thought sickened her.

"Okay, let's do it again!" The wedding planner clapped her hands together and surveyed the small crowd like a priest appealing to his congregation. "From the top. Ledger, we'll start with you bringing your mother down the aisle."

Alys felt a wave of nerves lap at her, which was ridiculous. How hard was it to put one foot in front of the other until she stood at the front row of chairs? Ledger dropped a kiss on the tip of Brooke's nose before coming back to stand beside Alys.

Fletcher hovered behind them, Claire and Josh at his elbow. Alys felt small in their shadows. The three of them had been there for her son when she walked out.

"Ready?" Ledger stepped closer to her and offered her a bland smile.

"Yeah." She gave herself a mental shake and linked her arm with her son's. Ledger patted her hand gently as they started walking. Words welled up inside her, so much she wanted to say to him. *I love you. I'm sorry. Please forgive me.*

She didn't deserve his forgiveness, and even if he were willing to give it to her, this wasn't the time to broach the subject with him, either. This was Brooke and Ledger's big weekend; Alys couldn't make it about herself. And yet, as they moved closer to the trellis and the minister who would marry them tomorrow, she felt her lungs expanding and her chest growing tighter. She needed to speak, to offer what little she could.

The moment passed as Ledger deposited her at the front row of chairs and Fletch stepped up beside her. Her body shook with the aftermath of need, of shutting down how badly she needed to say those words to her son, like she was gasping just to breathe. When Fletch glanced at her, she avoided his eyes and turned to watch the groomsmen escort the bridesmaids down the aisle. Hallie beamed at her as she took her spot in the line of attendants, and Alys felt a tiny thrill of hope that at least Hallie might walk away from this weekend in a better place than when she had arrived.

Tomorrow there would be musicians here, a trumpeter and a violinist. Tonight, Brooke and Ledger's friends, giddy with the excitement of the moment, sang and trilled awful renditions of the Bridal March as Brooke walked between Roark and Julia up the aisle. Still off after quieting those words that tried to claw their way out of her mouth, Alys flinched at the sharp needle of pain in her belly, her heart. Had things been different, she and Fletch might have walked Jade down an aisle somewhere to give her to a man who promised to love her.

Again, Ledge and Brooke stood facing each other, fingers linked. The minister flew through the rituals of the wedding ceremony, and for a moment, Alys was lost in the past, marrying Fletcher Holland. She could hardly see him for the stars in her eyes back then. She'd loved him blindly and promised him the rest of her life.

If she had known on that day that twenty-five years into their future, they would lose two of their three children in a tragic accident, would she still have married him? If she hadn't, if she hadn't taken his ring, if she hadn't said I do, the chronic heartache she carried now wouldn't exist. Time had not erased it. Running hadn't taken her far enough away from it. Whiskey didn't drown it.

If she could wipe out the past with a magic wand and recreate their lives to save them the loss, the suffering, would she do it?

No. Because she and Fletch had too much happy, too much love to pretend it never happened. Surprised to find herself near tears, Alys swallowed the thick emotion in her throat and dabbed at her eyes. When the rehearsal was over, Fletch waited to usher her away from the chairs. But instead of walking ahead of him, she remained at his side and reached for his hand.

Serving tables were set up a small distance away where members of the wedding party and guests could help themselves to hors d'oeuvre. Alys remained at Fletch's side, but she wasn't hungry, so she barely nibbled on her food. She managed to finish a maple-caramelized fig, but the bacon topping would surely make her regret it. Fletch, on the other hand, was apparently hungry, judging from the two figs, the shredded brussels sprout and ricotta toast, and almond tarts he piled on his small plate.

Mindful of the fact that she hadn't eaten much, and her stomach would surely give her fits after eating a piece of bacon, Alys sipped her wine. She wasn't entirely comfortable with Fletcher, not after the night they had spent together, after sabotaging the decent day with what she had said to him, but she would stay with the devil she knew. At least Fletch was a buffer between herself and Brooke and Ledger's guests that she didn't know.

As the last of the sunlight bled from the sky and dripped into the ocean, resort staff made their way around the gathering, inconspicuous and efficient, and began to clear away the empty plates and glasses. The party moved en masse to Howie's for an informal gathering with music and a cash bar. The reception itself would be on the main patio of the resort under what Alys hoped would be a sky full of stars.

"I think it's going to be a beautiful wedding," Claire announced as she approached Fletch and Alys. Fletch had claimed a table on the patio, and Alys had been relieved to sit for a moment. Her feet were tired in the wedge heels she wore, and the night before was still heavy around her neck, weighing her down.

"Of course it is." Fletch rolled his eyes. "Look at my son. He looks just like me."

"I think the wedding is the bride's show." Claire patted his chest and winked at Alys. "I meant this is a gorgeous venue."

"It is," Fletch agreed. He turned to Alys. "Want anything to drink?"

She wanted bourbon. Straight from the bottle. But saying so now would raise some eyebrows.

"Wine."

He nodded, but before he could head for the bar, someone was tapping a glass as if gearing up for an announcement or a toast. Alys swallowed a groan.

"So. Um." Ledger cleared his throat and looked around with a genuine smile at everyone gathered on the patio. "Brooke and I just wanted to say thank you for being here."

There were some catcalls and wolf whistles, presumably from Ledger's friends. Alys loved the color in Ledger's cheeks, the life in his eyes. Even if she had messed him up and created that sliver of darkness inside him, he could still find joy in his life with Brooke.

"Obviously, tomorrow is the big day," he continued, "but we figured we might be a little busy and forget something. So." His shrug and boyish grin tugged at Alys' heart. She remembered that look well, although she hadn't seen him wear it in a long time.

"We especially wanted to thank our families for being here." Brooke leaned into Ledger when he slipped his arm around her. "And especially our parents."

Alys climbed to her feet when Fletch reached for her. She hated being the center of attention even in the old days, and being called out like this made her uncomfortable. But Ledger and Brooke were now motioning to them to come and join them, and a waitress presented Ledger with a bottle of champagne, so there was no getting out of this. To her surprise, Julia took Alys' hand when they found themselves standing side by side with their children. Fletch and Roark shook hands.

"I don't know..." Ledger started, but his voice broke, and he tried again. "I don't know how many of you know this about me."

Alys ducked her head, afraid of what was coming. Julia squeezed her fingers.

"I was a twin," Ledge continued. Alys didn't have to look at him to know he was struggling to control himself. "I had a twin sister."

Fletch moved closer to Alys, hooking his arm around her shoulders.

"My twin and my younger brother were killed...in a car accident two years ago."

Alys sobbed softly and leaned, grateful for Fletch's support. She gasped for a breath and lifted her head to meet Ledger's eyes.

"I just want to say thank you to the woman who walked through hell with me to get me back on my feet." Ledger broke the eye contact and looked down at his fiancée. Alys pressed her lips together, determined to control herself. "I love you, Brooke."

Brooke murmured something to Ledger, and they shared a moment, and then Ledger looked back at the family and friends gathered around them.

"We wanted to include Jade and Kase this weekend."

Alys pulled her hand away from Julia and pressed her fist against her chest. Pain radiated through her ribs, up into her shoulder, and her arm.

"It's a..." Ledger blinked and swallowed hard. "It's still difficult. And I know it's hard for my parents. So, um...We thought we would do this here tonight, so that maybe..." He shook his head and stepped back, as if he couldn't go on.

"So maybe tomorrow will only be for happy tears," Brooke finished for him.

Alys watched them both look toward the building, the bar behind Claire and Josh. When she saw the big screen TV with Brooke and Ledger's engagement picture, her knees went weak. The video started, and while the music was soft and quiet, she found herself watching a live video, rather than the slideshow of still images she expected.

"What first attracted me to her? To Brooke?" Ledger grinned at the camera. "Her smile. I mean, she's beautiful, but her smile lights up a room. And if she's smiling, she's almost always laughing. I love to hear her laugh."

"Where did you meet her?"

Alys didn't recognize the voice that had asked the question. Or the room where Ledger sat on a dove gray leather sectional sofa. A vase of yellow and purple tulips graced an end table to Ledger's right. Ledge looked casual and comfortable in dark wash jeans and a white T-shirt.

"I met Brooke at a party. A graduation party for my boss's niece. She interned with us, so several of us at work were invited. Brooke and my boss' wife are friends."

"Did you talk much at the party? Did you ask her out?"

Ledger opened his mouth as if to answer, but he seemed shy suddenly and barked a nervous laugh instead. "I wanted to ask her out. I didn't, though. Not that day. We did talk to each other. We got into this discussion about salt on watermelon or not, and it led to a conversation about haiku poetry. And we ended up hanging out on the porch together all evening talking."

"Haiku poetry?"

That grin again. It tore Alys apart.

"Five. Seven. Five," Ledger explained, but he shook his head and waved the question away. "Brooke writes haiku, but that's another story."

"So, if you didn't ask her out, how did that happen?"

"Well, I walked her to her car that evening. And we were laughing. I mean, I was just a kid. And I was fascinated by her. She grabbed my hand and pulled out a pen and she said, if you're not gonna ask for my number, I'm gonna make sure you have it anyway. And she wrote her number on my arm. I called her the next day."

"Where did you take her? On your first date?"

"We had dinner at this little Italian place. Brooke wore a dress. Um...it was like a light bluish purple, and it was sleeveless and long, and she wore these sexy strappy sandals. She was this intoxicating mix of sweet and sexy, and I knew before that night was over, she was going to be the love of my life."

Alys flinched, but this time, she was thinking about Fletcher. She had known from the word go that Fletcher Holland was it for her. He worked for the city the summer he turned nineteen. Alys had walked out of the bank where she worked as a teller, and there he was in his neon yellow T-shirt and worn denim, hard hat, and reflective vest, holding a STOP sign in the middle of the street.

She had looked her fill, especially impressed with the way he wore denim. Worn but snug in the right places. She liked his ass, and later, after they had been dating for a while, she told him it was his ass that first attracted her to him. Fletch had turned his head as she crossed the street and let out a whistle that would ordinarily have earned him a flying bird. Instead, she peeked at him over her shoulder and looked away without a smile.

He had been there every day that summer. Even when his job site moved, Fletch showed up at the bank every day when she punched out. She played hard to get, but she was hooked from day one.

"How did you propose?" The interviewer asked Ledger on screen. "Or can you tell us?"

Ledge laughed and held his hands up as if to defend himself. "Hey! Her parents are watching this video." More laughter, and then Ledger continued, "It was after...the accident. It was rough. There were days I didn't want to get out of bed. Brooke was there. Through all of it. She reminded me she loved me. And she told me more than once Jade and Kase wouldn't want me to...throw my life away with the darkness. So. I don't know. It didn't happen overnight. But...I—no. We. We got through it. And we were in Florida. Disneyland. Brooke's a Disney girl."

"You proposed on a ride?"

"No. I actually planned to ask her during the fireworks at the end of the day. I couldn't wait."

Alys had to smile. Ledger was the kid who had to wear his new shoes home. The kid who was so excited about a present he picked out for Fletcher for Father's Day, that he blurted it out over dinner that same night.

"We were having ice cream. Talking about going home and how it would be more fun just to stay. Never go back to real life. Brooke was laughing, saying that she would hang out with the princesses, and I blurted it out. Asked her to marry me, and she just looked at me like she wasn't sure she heard me right. So, I got down on my knee and got the ring out of my pocket."

"Were you worried she would say no?"

"No." Ledger shook his head. He sounded so certain, Alys was intrigued. Because according to Brooke, a month later, she gave him the ring back.

"One more question, Ledger."

Ledger nodded.

"What do you look forward to most in your life with Brooke?"

"Just being with her. Every day. Knowing that every morning when I wake up, she's going to be right there beside me."

The screen went black, and there was a smattering of applause. Fletch, his arm still around Alys' shoulders, pulled her close and kissed the top of her head.

This time when the screen came to life, the camera was on Brooke. She sat cross-legged in a blue chair with bright yellow oversized cushions. Skinny jeans and an oversized sweatshirt, her hair pulled back in a messy twist, she was every All-American boy's dream.

"What do you love most about Ledger?"

Brooke laughed and covered her mouth for a second. "No easy warm up questions, huh? Ledge got all of those, didn't he?" She sighed and stared just past the camera, as if she was studying Ledger himself. "I love that even though he's an adult with a real job, he loves to come home and shoot baskets. I love that he's creative in the kitchen. If I want to make spaghetti, and I don't have sauce, Ledger loves to throw stuff together and make his own. I love that he laughs at Bugs Bunny cartoons, and I love that he's always ready and looking for an adventure."

Brooke shrugged and blinked at the camera.

"I guess it's the boy he is inside the man," she said softly. "He's tough, but he's soft. He's witty, but he's charming. He's responsible, but he's fiercely possessive. He has a good game face, but God, have you seen that smile? That dimple?" She laughed.

"Easy, tiger, not that kind of video."

Brooke's cheeks flushed a deep pink, and she covered her face, but she was laughing.

"What's your favorite memory with him?"

"Oh man. C'mon. That's so hard."

"Your first date?"

"Is that what he said?"

"I'm asking you."

Brooke nibbled on her lip for a moment. "I guess...maybe our first kiss."

"Why?"

"We had spent the day with Ledger's sister and brother. Um. I didn't get the chance to know them well, but we were at the park, playing frisbee golf. And I loved seeing the way Ledger was with them. I liked the way he and Jade—his sister—teased each other all the time. She cut him no slack, and I loved it. I think Jade and I would have been good friends. I...um...Ledge always said he and Kase were like oil and water, that they argued too much, but that day, Ledger was helping Kase with how to release the frisbee so it would carry further. And I remember thinking wow, this guy's gonna be great with kids."

"When did he kiss you? On the frisbee course?"

Brooke grinned. "No. When he took me home that night."

"If you could change one thing about Ledger, what would it be?"

"I wish I could take away the grief. I know I can't, and I know that kind of grief just speaks to how close Ledger was with his siblings. But I hate that he carries that sadness inside all the time."

"What do you look forward to most in your life with Ledger?"

Brooke smiled that radiant smile Ledger had just talked about.

"Having babies. Loving him every day. Growing old with him."

Fletch turned to face Alys when the screen went black again. "You okay?"

She sniffled and ducked her head to rest on his shoulder.

"Yeah." She wiggled her arms up between their bodies to dab at her eyes.

"Champagne, ma'am?"

She turned her head toward the voice and took the proffered flute. Fletch took one, too. Before either of them could speak, the music and the video started again. Alys glanced at the TV over Fletch's shoulder, freezing with dread when a baby photo of Brooke appeared. She was cute and bald and smiling, but Alys knew more pictures of Brooke would follow, pictures of her first step or her learning to ride her bike or a dance recital and high school graduation, and then when those pictures were done, pictures of Ledger would flash on the screen, and nearly every damned childhood picture of Ledger included Jade.

"I can't do this," she whispered.

"What?" Fletch asked, but he turned toward the TV screen, and Alys felt more than heard his grunt.

"Did you give them pictures?" she asked him.

"No."

Either Ledger or Ledger and Brooke had gone to Fletch's house—her old house—and dug through their photo albums, or Claire had done it for them. Irrational anger, envy, roared through her body like a freight train. They had no right to dig through her belongings, to look at photos and remember good times, when Alys couldn't bring herself to do it.

"Allie." Fletch tightened his hold on her.

"I can't."

"Please? I want to see them. Please do this with me?"

He held her close, his arms around her protectively, as Brooke changed on the screen and finally, she was grown, and there was newborn Ledger. The second picture was of Alys in the hospital, holding the twins in her arms, Fletch leaning over the side of her bed to be included. Alys' mother had taken the picture. For a moment, Alys focused on that. The fact that she had lost her mother too young and lost her father six years later.

But the next picture was of the twins as toddlers, in snowsuits and stocking caps, playing with Fletch in the snow. Alys swayed on her feet. Jade's snowsuit was pink and the ball on her stocking cap was white, and her little face was screwed up in a near wink, the sun so bright on the snow, she could hardly see.

The twins on their fifth birthday. Ledger riding his bike.

Ledger as a soccer goalie. The twins with Kase, when she and Fletch brought him home as a newborn.

Fletch held her. Pressed so close together, she felt his body shudder a time or two, heard his sharp intake of breath. When the pictures changed to older shots where Jade and Kase looked more like they did when they lost them, Fletch leaned his cheek on her head. Alys looked away from the screen when the picture changed to Jade and Ledger in their caps and gowns from college graduation. They had gone to different schools, but Alys had insisted on the pictures of them together. Their caps soared in the air, their smiles identical, even if their faces weren't.

Alys pressed her face into Fletch's neck and squeezed her eyes closed.

"You okay?" she whispered. He didn't speak, but she felt him move against her and shake his head.

Chapter Twenty

THE VIDEO STARTED AGAIN. DREAD, PANIC LAPPED at her like flames. The kids planned to let it play on a loop, so anyone who missed the interviews would see them. So everyone could ooh and aww over the photos. So anyone who knew Jade and Kase could remember them fondly.

And break into a million little pieces and fall to the patio, only to be walked on and then swept away at the end of the night.

"I need some air."

Still tucked away in Fletch's arms, she pushed at him now, desperate to breathe.

"Allie."

"Fletch, I can't breathe."

"Allie, go to Ledger." Fletch's gruff whisper was like a round of bullets in her chest, freezing her lungs.

"I can't." She shook her head only slightly, paralyzed now at the thought of approaching her son.

"Please."

Their eyes met. Rather than look away, Alys stared into Fletch's deep blue eyes, reading the pain, the sorrow she had always refused to wade too far into. Of course he was right. Any normal mother, any mother who had a heart, would go to her son now and offer comfort.

She wasn't normal, though, was she? She sure as hell wasn't a good mother.

A flash of Fletch, the breakdown in the shower, sent a shiver through her. Fletcher thought she left him because she blamed him. Brooke had told her Ledger blamed himself.

She broke the eye contact when she thought of Fletch making love to her last night. Her trepidation about letting go, feeling good in his arms. Laughing with him this morning when he suggested celebrating their grandbaby by touching her in such an intimate way—something she hadn't allowed him to do through the night.

She heard Fletch's sigh. Noticed from the corner of her eye the way his shoulders drooped. Disappointment. He was disappointed in her. She'd hurt him earlier, but right now, disappointing him was somehow worse. Because this was about their son, not their relationship.

Maybe if she went to Ledger now, talked to him, hugged him —something—maybe she could salvage that relationship.

Fletch clearly expected her to scurry away from the party to hide. Maybe to drink. Instead, Alys handed her glass to a waitress as she walked by, smoothed her damp palms over her hips and turned to search Ledger out. Standing with Brooke and her parents, he held a champagne flute. He was looking at

Roark, as if listening to him, but Alys saw the absent look on his face.

Was he thinking about Jade? Kase? The frisbee golf outing? Or was he reliving the night of the accident? Blaming himself again.

Alys took a deep breath of late summer air and let the briny smell of the ocean fill her. Her legs were heavy, but she managed a step. And then another. By the third step, Ledger noticed her and jerked his face her way to watch her approach. Brooke looked her way, too, and stepped aside immediately.

"I'm sorry," Ledger started before she could say anything. "I didn't mean to upset you and Dad, but I needed to acknowledge—"

"Ledge." His name was broken on her lips. She coughed softly and cleared her throat, but when she couldn't control herself, when she couldn't say more, she simply rushed the last few steps and reached for him.

Tall like Fletch, he had to lean to hug her. Even in her heels, Alys was on her tiptoes, arms sliding up over his shoulders. They held onto each other for a long time, no words exchanged. Tears wet her face; Ledger's body trembled against hers.

"I'm sorry," she whispered at his neck. With one hand still over his shoulder, she moved the other to pat his chest and then grip his upper arm. "I'm so sorry I abandoned you."

Ledger was talking, too, *sorry* and *his fault* and *forgive me*. His words wedged into her under her skin like a file under a fingernail, shoved deep and painful. She wondered briefly who was watching them and wished they were somewhere private.

"I don't blame you, Ledge." She shook her head. "I have never blamed you for what happened."

"You should, though," he argued. "Kase called me. It should have at least been me and not Jade."

"And you think that would be any easier for me and Dad? Losing you instead of Jade?"

"I'm bigger than Kase," he mumbled. "I could have taken the keys from him."

"It's not your fault," Alys insisted.

Ledge took a step back and shoved his hands in his pockets. He looked around the patio, his eyes bloodshot and glassy.

"Look." She moved her hand from his arm and reached up to cup his face. "This isn't a good time to do this. Not with your guests here. This is your wedding weekend, Ledger. And you have an incredible woman to do your life with. So, celebrate now. Okay?"

The half-shrug answer sent a jolt of panic through her. Were he and Brooke on the outs again?

"Ledge? Is everything okay with you and Brooke?" She tipped her head.

Their eyes met again.

"With the baby?"

"She told you?"

Alys nodded.

"We're fine." He frowned and shook his head. Alys waited patiently for him to continue, to say more. She dropped her hand. when he pinched the bridge of his nose and breathed deeply for a moment. "I just..."

"What? Just say it."

"Am I ever gonna see you again? After the wedding?"

Maybe they were at the rehearsal dinner for her man-child's wedding, but in that moment, Alys saw the five-year-old boy inside the man. Ledger, asking if he could have a cookie even though she was fixing dinner. Ledger, asking if he could go to his friend's house for a sleepover. Ledger, telling her he asked a girl to homecoming and needed a new suit for the dance.

Ledger, confessing to her and Fletch that he got a speeding ticket.

That little boy was there in his face now. Ledger, asking his mother if she was going to abandon him again.

She stopped herself before blurting *of course*. Or *absolutely*. Something so strong sounded fake, the same sorts of answers she had been giving him the last couple of years. Lies intended to string him along and get him off her back.

"Yes."

He stared at her silently as if trying to decide if he should trust her.

She said it again. "Yes."

He gasped and looked around as if he was embarrassed to get emotional. But he gave her a curt nod. "Okay." She watched him walk away and prayed that he was simply walking out for a second to catch his breath. That he would come back to Brooke and not leave her alone at their party.

"Thank you."

Alys closed her eyes when Brooke stepped up beside her and linked her fingers through hers. She swallowed a ridiculous jab of anger. She didn't want to be thanked for loving her son. Loving, protecting her child should be primal. Instead, she had withheld her love for him and walked away, leaving him to battle his grief on his own.

"Give him a minute." She squeezed Brooke's hand and then dropped it and walked away. Careful not to follow Ledger, Alys slipped away from the crowd, too. Not to run away. But to breathe. Process.

Remember.

She had forgotten the way Jade's right eye crinkled when she smiled big. She had forgotten that Jade streaked her hair with pink when she was fourteen. She had forgotten that Kase used to follow Ledger around the yard when they were younger, all but begging his big brother to throw a ball with him. She had forgotten that Kase's smile was a little crooked, that the left side of his mouth always climbed a bit higher than the right.

She had even forgotten things about Ledger. And that was no one's fault but her own.

How had she forgotten so much about her babies?

What kind of mother shoved all her memories away, good and bad, because she was afraid to hurt?

"Hey."

A few steps down the path in front of Howie's, Fletch caught up to her. Alys glanced at him, but she said nothing.

"I'm proud of you."

"Don't." She shook her head.

"Allie." He sounded exasperated. Alys pushed her hair back from her face and smoothed her fingers under her eyes.

"Don't, Fletch. You shouldn't be proud of me. Brooke shouldn't thank me. Please? You have to just...you have to let me work through this."

"Claire told me you admitted to thinking about suicide."

Alys rolled her eyes. "I didn't think of it as admitting anything. And yes, I imagined killing myself a hundred different ways, a hundred different times."

"Alys."

"And I still do," she said quietly. "Maybe I will forever."

"I don't want to lose you, too."

She stepped away from him when he put his arm around her.

"Don't." She stopped walking. "Fletch, last night was..."

"Don't say it was a mistake," he pleaded. "Look, I get it." His voice grew a bit louder, heavy with frustration. "Okay, maybe you don't blame me for what happened, but for whatever reason, you don't love me anymore. I get that, Allie. I'm not gonna stalk you, for God's sake. And it's not my pride stopping me. Because I would get down on my knees and beg you to take me back."

Uncomfortable with his honesty, Alys closed her eyes.

"I'm not stupid. Maybe last night was closure for you. Maybe it was your pity for me. Maybe—"

"Jesus, Fletch," she groaned. "It wasn't pity. And it sure as hell wasn't closure."

Hands in his pockets, Fletch dropped his head back and groaned.

"I don't know what it was. I don't know what I feel. I'm not saying it was a mistake."

"Then what?"

"It was..." She huffed a quick breath and dropped her gaze to the ground between them. "It was perfect, and perfect doesn't fit with how I feel inside. So, I don't know how to process it."

"I don't know what that means for us."

"Do you know why I would never kill myself?"

When he didn't answer, she peeked at him. He shrugged and arched his eyebrows.

"It would be too easy," she said simply. "For me. I know I've been horrible to you and Ledge. To Claire. And I'm so sorry. I really, truly am sorry for hurting you. For abandoning Ledger when he needed me."

"But?" Fletch prodded her.

"But that doesn't mean I know where to go from here. I don't know how to be happy anymore, Fletch. Because any time I feel good, I feel sick. I feel guilty."

"So being with me makes you feel sick."

She met his eyes and bit her lip but said nothing.

"So, last night, when we made love...Did you fake it? Were you physically ill when I was inside you?"

"No." She shook her head. "No. You took me away from all of it." She swallowed hard. "And that's the problem. I'm not sure

I can deal with that. I'm not sure I deserve to be happy, to feel good when our babies will never feel anything again."

"So, you're gonna be a martyr? You're gonna hole up alone for the rest of your life. Because you feel like living is a betrayal to Jade and Kase?"

She shrugged. Putting it that way sounded wrong. Arrogant. Even judgmental, as if she found fault with Fletch for being able to move on.

"I'm saying I don't know, Fletch." She tipped her head to study his face. When she blinked, tears streaked her face. "I just need some space."

"Now you're asking for space," he mumbled. "What do you want? Do I need to move my stuff to Claire and Josh's room?"

"I'm not talking about...physical space. I'm not talking about tonight. Tomorrow. I'm talking about us. About what happens in the future."

"Can I ask you one question?"

"What?"

"Were you happy with Iva?"

"I was...okay. Never happy. Iva's illness gave me a purpose. Being at home with you? Around Ledger?" She shook her head. "It was a daily reminder of everything we lost."

"And so how? How did you just stop loving me?"

"Fletch." She rubbed her face, exhausted from the conversation, dreading that she had to return to the party and pretend everything was okay.

"Because I could use that magic right about now. I would really like to not have to wake up in love with you every day."

"There's no magic." Tears streaked her face, but she made no move to wipe them away this time. "I still love you, Fletch. I'm never gonna not be in love with you."

Chapter Twenty-One

FLETCH MADE COFFEE WHILE ALYS SHOWERED. When he brought her a cup, he lingered for a moment in the doorway of the bathroom. Alys, in her bra and panties, didn't say a word. They had slept together again last night, even after the video and the harsh, honest conversation. Fletch had tried to gather his things quietly when they returned to the suite. It wasn't late, but Alys was emotionally drained. They moved through the living area to the bedroom, a barefoot Alys carrying her shoes, and Fletch unbuttoning his shirt as they walked.

When she emerged from the bathroom, ready to climb into bed, she found him with his shorts on, his pillow tucked under his arm, ready to slink out to sleep on the couch. Because the evening had left her feeling lonely, she wanted him with her. Because the pictures and memories, the conversations with Ledger and Fletcher had left her raw and exposed, she couldn't find the words to tell Fletcher that. Instead, she simply tugged the pillow from him, tossed it back to the bed, and pressed close to him.

"Are you sure?" he asked her. She nodded, tugging him into the bed. She wasn't sure, though, and they lay in the darkness, curled together, but worlds apart. Alys drifted off to sleep in his arms, woke once still pressed against his warm, hard body. She snuggled closer, overcome with emotion when Fletch moved in his sleep, tightened his hold around her, and murmured her name. When she awoke the second time, she had been dreaming about him, about his touch, and she had reached without thought to stroke her hand down his belly to cup him in her hand.

He was awake instantly, hard in her hand, and shifting to slide her over so she could straddle him. She made love to him, riding him, boldly taking what she needed in the darkness, surprised at the lack of guilt she felt over it once dawn lit their room.

"You're beautiful without all of that," he told her.

Alys paused in the act of smoothing foundation over her face. She met his eyes in the mirror and snorted softly.

"Fletch, I look like a has-been alcoholic," she told him. "I'll probably have to pay for the bags under my eyes on the flight home."

He sauntered into the room and stood behind her, careful to leave plenty of space between them.

"Okay, I'll give you that it's been a rough few days, and you've cried." He shrugged and grinned at her in the mirror. "But you're still beautiful, and…"

"And?" She turned to him and rested her butt on the counter.

"This is gonna sound selfish."

She shrugged as if inviting him to lash out.

"I'm glad you cried."

Uncertain how to take what he said, she nibbled on her lip and stared at him silently. Finally, she turned her back to him and washed her hands.

"You never let me see you break," he reminded her. "When the kids...after the accident. Maybe you didn't blame me for losing them, but you never trusted me to love you through it."

Alys picked up her cup and took a sip.

"You're right," she whispered over the top of her cup. "I didn't."

Apparently surprised that she had agreed so quickly, Fletch seemed dumbfounded. He stared at her for several long moments and finally stirred.

"I'll get out of your way—"

"You don't have to."

She spoke quietly, so as not to give away how her heart was crashing in her chest. Her need to be near him.

"What if I told you watching you makes me so hard my dick hurts?"

She met his eyes in the mirror again and smiled sadly.

"How old is Trish?"

But Fletch only shook his head. "I liked her. I really did. But you have always been the woman to make me crazy. In every way possible."

Alys looked away to root in her cosmetics bag for her eyeliner.

"What did you get them?"

"What?"

"Wedding present," she said, eyes still on the bag. "For Brooke and Ledger."

"Oh." He drank from his own cup. "Just giving them cash. Put a check in the card."

She nodded. "Me, too."

"I hope they make it," he announced, and Alys decided now wasn't the time to tell him they had called the wedding off twice.

"I do, too, Fletcher. I want Ledger to be happy."

"I know." He put his cup down and glanced at the shower. "Do you want a boy or a girl?"

"What?"

"Do you want our first grandbaby to be a boy or a girl?"

"Grandbaby," she repeated. "Good grief, how are we old enough to be grandparents?"

Fingers of one hand pulling her skin taut, Alys lined her eye in charcoal gray.

"We've been through a lot together."

She nodded.

"Not all bad."

Stunned at his comment, she turned to him, one eye lined.

"I never said it was all bad, and do not make me cry again. Not now. I have a wedding to go to in a few hours."

"Allie?"

"Hmm?" She turned her attention back to the mirror to work on her left eye.

"When we leave here."

She jerked her eyes to meet his again in the mirror and waited.

"Look, I mean, I'm not asking for another chance. I just...Will we talk? I love you so much; I just need you in my life. Any way you feel comfortable being a part of it."

Alys finished her left eye and tossed the pencil back in her bag.

"I would like that, Fletch," she said softly.

She turned to look at him, but neither of them moved. Finally, he nodded and cleared his throat. Looked at the shower again.

"Go ahead." She nodded to the shower.

"You sure?"

"Actually." Alys took a step closer to him. "Let me help."

"You just got your hair dry," he reminded her.

"Not in the shower." She yanked at the waistband of his shorts and slipped her hand inside his briefs.

"Maybe we could be friends with benefits?" he suggested as she closed her fingers around him.

"Not to beat a dead horse, but a guy like you can find something better for friends with benefits."

Fletch tugged at her hand until she let go of him. He took her hand in his and leaned closer to kiss her.

"Is this okay?"

"Kissing me?"

"You're putting on makeup."

"Just don't slobber on me."

His lips hovered close to hers; Alys could almost feel his smile.

"Alys."

"Fletcher?"

"Where's your ring?"

She looked down as his fingers traced her right hand.

"What?"

"Iva's ring?"

Alys swallowed hard. "I took it off yesterday," she whispered. "Before we went to the rehearsal."

"You weren't wearing it last night? When we made love?"

She shook her head.

"Where's your wedding ring?"

"At home."

"Promise me you'll never get rid of it."

"Fletch." She squinted her eyes and shook her head. "Of course I wouldn't get rid of my ring. I could give it to our granddaughter someday."

He kissed her again, a soft, sweet kiss that left her aching for more.

✦

BRILLIANT BLUE SKIES PROVIDED THE BACKDROP FOR Ledger and Brooke's wedding. Alys had to agree with Claire;

the Kahalina Bluffs Resort was a beautiful venue. But everything about this wedding was beautiful in Alys' eyes. Even the fact that Brooke had given Ledge the ring back, that they had called the wedding off just seven months ago. In Alys' mind, it spoke to the fact that they were desperately in love and willing to do the work to make their relationship last. Amazing to Alys, considering the example she had set for Ledger.

Today's tears were all happy. Alys' heart and mind were still crowded with sorrow, with memories of Jade and Kase, with grief and guilt, but she was present in Ledger and Brooke's happiness, and she allowed herself to be part of that. Brooke's dress was simple, yet stunning, the white satin flowing into a voluminous skirt, intricate beadwork on the bodice, with a white sash that accentuated Brooke's slender waist.

Alys wondered how far along she was.

Ledger was elegant in his charcoal-colored suit and the forest green tie that matched the bridesmaid's dresses. She had worried that seeing her son in a suit would throw her back to the funeral, but this was different. He was a grown man now, solid and strong, as she had discovered when she hugged him last night. His broad shoulders were proud today, where they had been hunched with misery at the funerals. He wore a smile today, and he only had eyes for his bride.

Their vows, like their attire, were classic and simple, and yet they still brought tears to Alys' eyes. Judging from Julia and Claire dabbing at their eyes, they were moved, too. When the minister announced them as Mr. and Mrs. Ledger and Brooke Holland, Alys swayed on her feet, but Fletch's arm around her steadied her.

A formal dinner was served at Calliope, and Alys was happy to be seated with Fletch, Claire, and Josh. She tried to listen to their conversations, but she was drawn to Brooke and Ledger, comforted by their love, their joy. Hallie appeared happy, too, talking animatedly with Brooke's friends.

The thought of going home tomorrow put a pall over the day, so she chased it away anytime it ventured to mind. Outside of Palos Verdes, Alys still lived alone in Iva's rambling house; Fletch still lived alone in the home they had shared as a family, and her babies were still gone. She could sell Iva's place. She had considered it through the night, after making love with Fletch. If she did sell it, she would donate the profit to a cause or causes Iva believed in. The American Cancer Society. Mental health or suicide prevention. Alys would carry Iva's friendship, her memory with her forever, but she didn't need or want her money.

If she sold the house, she wasn't sure where she would go. What if rushing back to the house with Fletch proved to be a mistake?

The first dance was sweet and fun. Ledger twirled his bride around, both of them looking insanely happy. Alys couldn't help but remember her first dance with Fletch at their reception. She had mentally prepared herself to dance with her son, so she stepped into his arms with a smile on her face.

"You clean up pretty good, Ledger Holland," she told him.

He laughed softly, eyes on Brooke.

"Congratulations, Ledge." She patted his chest again.

"Thanks, Mom." He turned his attention to her.

"When you get back from your honeymoon, maybe we could get coffee."

"Yeah?" His grin gripped her heart and squeezed.

"Maybe I'll buy you lunch."

"I thought about what you said."

"What did I say?" She looked up at him, heart in her throat.

"About never blaming me."

"And?"

"I know you didn't blame me, Mom. But." He shrugged. Alys watched his throat as he struggled for a moment to control his emotions. "But you taught me better than to ignore someone when they needed help. And I ignored Kase. Because I wanted to talk to Brooke."

"Sweetheart." Alys shook her head. She stared at him boldly. "You were just a kid yourself, and you had no idea what would happen. Dad and I were going to lose someone that night. Maybe that was fate. Maybe it was God." She shrugged. "I don't know. Yes, I miss Jade and Kase every day. And I've been so neglectful of you, but I do thank God every day that you're alive."

"Mom?"

"Hmm?"

"You're not angry with Brooke, are you? She told me she said some awful things to you—"

"Ledger, I needed to hear the ugly truth from Brooke. I'm not angry." She pushed up to her tiptoes and kissed his cheek. "I'm grateful to her."

There was more dancing, and this time, Alys enjoyed herself. She tucked Jade and Kase in her heart, promising them and herself to grieve again tomorrow, but she chose to be fully present in Ledger and Brooke's celebration. She had missed far too much time with them already.

"You guys have been burning up the sheets, haven't you?"

Alys looked at Claire over the top of her wine glass.

"What makes you say that?"

"Something's changed between you guys."

The ocean whispered around them. A soft breeze played in Alys' hair. Claire studied her so intensely, Alys feared she would read her mind and memories and know exactly what she and Fletch had been doing at night. Behind them, just inside, Ledger and Brooke and their guests did the Cha-Cha Slide.

"I never meant to hurt him," Alys said rather than giving Claire a straight answer.

"I know that."

"Do you?"

"We grieved, too, Allie," Claire reminded her. "Don't we all lash out in our grief?"

Claire was right. Alys drew in a deep breath and nodded.

"I guess so."

"Are you gonna go back to him?"

"I don't know, Claire," Alys mumbled. "I just need some time."

"You're gonna break all of our hearts again if you walk away again."

"Please don't push me. I just need space."

Claire's nostrils flared when she breathed, but she nodded.

"I'm scared," she admitted. "For you."

"I shouldn't have said that to you." Alys looked away. "I promise you I'm not going to hurt myself, Claire. The best way to punish myself is to consider all the easy ways of walking away from the pain. And not giving myself the option to do any of them."

"I don't even get why you need to punish yourself, but isn't it time to let it go? To move on?"

"I asked you—"

"I'm not pressuring you about Fletch," Claire insisted. "I'm saying be happy, Allie. Whatever it takes, I want you to be happy."

Alys nodded after a long moment of silence. "Thank you."

"Love you," Claire told her. "I do. Josh and I both love you. No matter where you end up."

"I know." Alys nodded. She draped her arm around Claire and pulled her close. "I love you guys, too."

Epilogue

A MONTH AFTER THE WEDDING, ALYS MET WITH A real estate agent to discuss Iva's house and finally made the decision to put the house up for sale. The decision left her somewhat relieved, but also guilty, as if she were deserting Iva.

Even though it was what Iva would have wanted.

She had told her that once. They had become fast friends, sharing appetizers over drinks and secrets because of too many drinks. Alys had confided all the ugly feelings after the accident: the guilt, the hate, the exhaustion, the need to walk away from all of it, her flirtation with suicide, her jealousy when Fletch started seeing Trish. Iva had shared with Alys the story of her first relationship—that one with the boy she had gone to college with. She had confessed to never feeling right with him, never being attracted to him as other girls talked about, and not enjoying sex with him. She told Alys about coming out to her parents, her fears that they would be disappointed in her. Though they had been shocked, they had accepted Iva's declaration with grace and told her they wanted her to be happy.

Iva told Alys one night over drinks that she was in love with her. That she expected nothing in return, although she hoped her admission didn't scare Alys away from their friendship. As Iva's disease progressed, Alys put down roots and nursed her, as well as remaining her friend. The few small sexual things notwithstanding, Iva simply told Alys she would never be able to give her heart to anyone else, because she was still in love with Fletch.

Iva had asked Alys to promise she would go back to Fletch and try to make it work when she was gone. It was one more thing Alys couldn't give her.

Now here she was, parking her car in the street in front of the old house she and Fletcher had shared. She cut the engine, but her butt remained rooted to the seat. She was scared. No, more than that. Alys was terrified to take the next step. The gray-sided two-story house was daunting without resident ghosts, but now, memories of Jade and Kase in every damned room, Alys wasn't sure she could set foot inside.

She damned sure wasn't ready to do it today.

But she had come anyway.

The realtor was showing Iva's house. Alys looked at her watch. She had planned to look at a condo while the realtor was at Iva's. And yet, when she got in the car, she had simply driven and ended up here.

She opened the car door and put one foot out on the ground. Fingers curled around the steering wheel, she hesitated. Looked back at the driveway and remembered the night Kase and Zoey left the house together. The night Kase and Jade left the family.

With a deep breath, she forced herself to get out of the car. Fletcher might not even be home. Then she could get back in the car and get the hell away from here.

She hadn't talked to him since the day after the wedding. He had offered to change his flight, so they could be together. She asked him not to. They parted company in the resort lobby. A quick hug and soft, chaste kiss.

Alys held it together through the flight, but once home, once at Iva's, in the room she had claimed as her own, she had crawled into bed alone and cried for days.

There had been a few texts to and from Fletch. They teased a bit. Never spoke about the love they had made and left behind again in Palos Verdes. She missed him. The texts weren't enough.

But she wasn't sure what she wanted or needed. And she didn't want to lead him on.

The windows were open, but there was no sound from the house. Alys shivered in her light jacket, waiting on the porch for Fletch to answer the door. September had started out hotter than the devil, but the past few days had turned chilly. She smiled to herself when she remembered the fluffy sage green baby blanket she had found yesterday for Brooke and Ledger. Brooke had started showing almost overnight. She was only four months along, and her baby bump was cute and tiny still, but it was there, and every time she saw it, Alys thrilled more to the idea of being a grandma.

When Fletch didn't answer the door, she turned away, stewing over the disappointment and angry with herself for feeling that way. She had half hoped the whole way up the walk that no one would answer.

She heard something from the backyard as she stepped off the porch, so instead of heading to her car, she turned right and meandered further down the driveway. Her eyes swept the side of the house, took in the rose bushes and the welcome mat at the back door. Fletch's truck was in the garage, a light on in the back over his worktable. But still no sign of Fletch himself.

The hammering noise came again, drawing her attention to the treehouse Fletch had built for the kids. Through the small door, she could see his work boots. Alys lifted her own boot clad foot and started climbing the ladder.

"What're you doing?" she asked when she reached the top rung.

"Hey." Fletch took a nail from between his teeth and stared at her, clearly surprised to see her.

"What're you doing?" she repeated.

"Um." He looked around the floor of the house and back at her. "Replacing a few of the boards. They're a little bit rotten."

"Why?"

Fletch shrugged his eyebrows and sat back on his knees.

"I guess...in case Ledge and Brooke's little one is ever around here."

"Of course, the baby will be around here." She rolled her eyes. "Might be a while before he or she can climb up here, though."

His sheepish grin was a torpedo in her heart.

"Something to do," he mumbled. She nodded and looked around the platform, remembering the kids playing up here.

Somehow Jade was always the boss. The memory brought a smile to her lips. "What're you doing here?"

Alys jerked her gaze back to Fletcher.

"Looking at houses," she answered.

"Yeah? Thinking about a treehouse this time?"

She smiled, but nervous now, she looked away. What if he wouldn't want her to come back home?"

"Fletch."

"What, Allie?"

"Can I come home?"

Fletch put the hammer down and crawled toward her. He took her hand and helped her climb over the last step. She sat beside him and leaned close when he put his arm around her.

"Lots of memories in that house, Allie. You sure you're ready for that?"

"I could just stay out here until we're all ready."

"We should name the treehouse," he announced.

"Yeah?"

"Holland House."

"Mmm." She nodded. Fletch kissed her forehead.

"You like it?"

"I love it."

"Have you seen Ledge lately?" Fletch asked her.

Alys shivered as a strong wind rustled through the leaves over their heads. Fletch rubbed his hand over her back.

"I had lunch with Brooke two days ago."

"Before or after her ultrasound?"

"Before. Why?"

"They're having twins."

"What?" Alys laughed softly.

"We're gonna have a Felicity Jade and a Daniel Kase."

"Wow."

"You okay with that?"

"I guess it depends," she answered.

"On what?"

"If we're gonna grandparent together." Leaning closer, she tipped her head up to look at him.

"Guess we're okay with that," he said simply.

Alys closed her eyes as he brushed his lips over hers.

"We should get married again," she decided.

"We should what?"

"Before the grandbabies arrive. So it's proper."

Fletch patted his pockets down and pulled his phone from the chest pocket of his flannel shirt.

"Who're you calling?"

"A priest," he answered.

"Yeah? You have someone on speed dial?" She grinned and quirked an eyebrow at him.

"I don't." He lowered the phone to his lap, still smiling.

"You could just sit right here and hold me for a while. And we could call someone later."

***

Turn the page to read Chapter One of Truth Is, The Williams Legacy, Book 1

Truth Is: The Williams Legacy Book 1

Drab, pale gray daylight inside and outside. If it wasn't for the watery lines from raindrops on the windows, she might not have been able to distinguish what was inside the bedroom where she slept and what was outside in the frigid January morning. The raindrops and the little flicks of ice on the window as Mother Nature tried to decide if she wanted to wreak havoc with rain or ice took her back to her childhood. When she and Olivia would ride in the backseat of their parents' Chevy Malibu station wagon (an '83 model, if she remembered correctly, plain white, which at seven made her jealous of the people who drove the *classy* kind with wood grain panels), and rain drops the size of the Hope diamond battered the windshield, and her dad had to lean forward and squint and drive thirty in a fifty mile an hour zone, and she and Olivia would draw hearts and write their initials in the steam on the windows in the back.

And their mom would yell at them.

Of course she would yell at them. Who liked washing windows, especially the very back windows of a station wagon, when you had to climb way back into the car to reach them, and then they streaked, and you never got them really clean...

Tired of the watery gray scenery, Ingrid flopped over to her back and rolled her head on her pillow to look at the clock. The ancient tiny alarm clock glowed turquoise numbers and had a missing line out of the second number so that right now instead of saying 5:02, it said something like 5:d2. Apparently, old habits died hard, and the setting didn't matter. She'd been tossing and turning for the better part of an hour, thinking about her dad and her sisters and brother and the funeral, and lying around and remembering particular moments from your dad's funeral tended to make the minutes crawl by, and so she guessed maybe she'd been awake since three.

She didn't particularly want to get out of bed, but there was no reason to stay in bed, either, except that she was at least warm under the sheets and comforter, and because the house was big and old, and she would freeze her ass off the second she threw the covers back. She groaned and sighed and covered her eyes with the heels of her hands. Rubbed them hard enough to see flecks of kaleidoscope colors on her eyelids, and though the colors were generally better than the gray in her room and outside her window, right now, anything reminiscent of her childhood sucked, (Didn't all kids put pressure on their eyeballs to make the magic kaleidoscope of colors appear on their eyelids?) and so she tossed the covers back and rolled over to climb to the edge of the full bed.

Did they even make full beds anymore? She didn't think so. Didn't remember seeing them when she'd gone furniture shopping with Julie when she and Rafe had redecorated Jayden's room, complete with a new queen-sized bed. This particular bed was old, maybe not as old as Ingrid herself, but old and surprisingly comfortable. At least until her eyes had popped open before daybreak and refused to close again.

Head pounding, Ingrid sat on the side of the bed for a minute. The braided rug on the floor was cold. She dreaded the thought of her feet hitting the hardwood floor at the end of the rug and leading all the way out to the threadbare carpet runner in the hall and down the stairs. She heaved another big sigh and then popped her neck. Considered turning on the lamp—also a relic from the eighties—coated in the dust that had begun to accumulate after her mother passed away six years ago, (Had it really been that long?) but in the end she didn't. She leaned forward, eyes on the rug, and looked for the socks she'd peeled off last night just before she'd climbed under the covers.

She yawned as she caught site of them and slipped off the bed. Squatted and grabbed them and then sat down again to pull them on. Helped a little, but honestly, she still felt like she'd slept in the tundra, and her teeth were thinking about chattering, though they hadn't started yet. Without looking, she grabbed her phone and moved quickly from her room to the hall. The house was silent, save for the age-old creaks and pops it made as it settled. Being that it had been in this same position, at this same address for a good sixty-some years, Ingrid thought it should have settled a long time ago, but then who was she to judge? She'd been living in her apartment in the suburbs for at least twelve years, and honestly, she hadn't settled yet, had she?

The hallway was a darker shade of gray than the bedroom where she'd slept. No windows, just six doorways. One door closed. She wondered if Amber was awake. She didn't care enough to even glance at the closed door as she passed it. Instead, she tiptoed by the room and stepped gingerly down the stairs, careful to sidestep the creaky spots they'd all memorized when they were teens going through the inevitable rebellious stage, sneaking out, coming home drunk or high or both or sneaking boys or girls up to their rooms after a date. *Well*. Ingrid had never done *that*. Olivia had on occasion, and she was pretty sure Amber had, but then a whole world existed between herself and Amber, and so really, she didn't know anything for certain about Amber, except that she was the baby of the family, which apparently entitled her to be a bitch.

Awake enough now to feel the tug toward the kitchen, the need for coffee, Ingrid stopped for a moment to look out the bay window to the street. It had snowed, apparently, during the few hours she'd slept, and it was still sort of spitting freezing rain, and right now, it was almost pretty: the narrow street in front of the house and the unblemished snow and the small icicles hanging from the roof of the porch. Ingrid felt a pull inside, like she'd strained a muscle, only it was sort of like a memory and a little bit of Christmas and her parents and home, and she ducked her head and rubbed her face with her fingertips and thought about the Christmas tree in the living room.

January fourteenth, and they hadn't gotten around to taking Dad's Christmas tree down. Sure, it was small-ish, and maybe it wouldn't take that long to do it, but Ingrid dreaded the thought of crawling through the attic and digging shit out just to put other shit away.

Then again, wasn't that why she was here? To dig shit out and get rid of it?

It'd be nice if her nephew and brother-in-law could come around and help out.

Headlights sliced through the steel-colored neighborhood outside the window, and Ingrid remembered she wanted coffee. *Well. Needed* coffee. And really, as much as she didn't want to deal with it, now would be a good time to check her email. Before Amber or Hadley was awake. Before Olivia sashayed through the back door with her navy paper *Beans, Leaves & Love* cup and her *kiss-my-ass* bossiness and told Ingrid to shut the damned laptop down and get off her ass and get to work.

Maybe a little light would take the edge off how blah she felt. But she wasn't ready to take the edge off anything; in fact, the edge actually felt like it was getting sharper. She decided to go with it, maybe even nurse it a little, and so she went through the motions of making coffee in that same gray light that fell through the kitchen window above the sink that had greeted her as dawn finally caught up to her earlier.

Dad's coffee maker had seen better days, and so while it did its thing with the water and the ground coffee, Ingrid stood with a towel and did her thing, which was to mop up the water that inevitably ended up puddled behind the machine, along the length of the counter. She did so absently, eyes on the gray morning, on the snow that barely dusted the ground but heaped impressively on the picnic table that she imagined hadn't been used in at least six years, and most likely, maybe even six before that.

She and Olivia used to climb the massive Maple tree that ruled the backyard like a big-assed king on an iron throne. If they were getting along, they'd climb the tree together and spy on the neighbor boys or gossip about the kids at school. If they weren't, one would climb and holler mean things down to the other, and now Ingrid wondered if Ezra and Amber ever climbed it when they were younger.

Sopping up the water on the counter with the dishtowel, Ingrid reached, without looking, to open the cabinet next to the window and grab a mug. She'd almost been delighted that first day she'd arrived last week—or had it been two weeks ago, now?—to find big, deep drinking stoneware mugs the color of cobalt blue in the cabinet. But then she'd had a flash of guilt to be so enamored of coffee mugs when she was here for her father's funeral.

Still. There was comfort in the act of pouring the coffee and adding just a small dash of the powdered creamer her niece had lectured her about that first day. *Trans fats. Unhealthy. Die young. Blah blah blah.* Ingrid stirred her coffee with the tiny silver coffee spoon that was always left on the counter by the coffee maker. She set it down again and picked up her mug without a thought as to where the spoon had come from and why it was always out, and she shuffled like a zombie to the big, oak dining table where the six of them used to sit for meals. Before after school jobs and college had gotten in the way of family. Before the weddings and careers had driven them away from family. Before death had stolen family away from them.

Watery gray light fell through windows all around the table. Ingrid's heart jumped a little and startled her when she saw her Mac on the table. She never left it out, unguarded. True, it was password protected, and she used random passwords, never cutesy passwords with a lover's name or an anniversary or anything as nauseating or predictable as that. Still. She hated that her Mac had been down on this table all night, where anyone else could have attempted to use it. Or snoop through it.

She'd been so tired, though. So tired and weary, and her bones had hurt, and her mind kept playing the funeral loop, and she'd wanted silence instead of her siblings' snipping at each other and the remembered conversations that could easily have been one, as everyone surrendered to default conversation at events such as weddings and funerals.

Wishing she had a blanket, or at least a robe, she sat at the head of the table and took a drink of her coffee. Cold seeped in through the windows, like gray had an actual temperature and it was maybe zero, and Ingrid shivered as she put her mug on the table and reached for her MacBook. She opened it and powered it up, typed her password in and then sat absently twisting the huge silver ring on the middle finger of her right hand.

Truth be told, she loved her MacBook more than any one person in her life, but she preferred it at home in her apartment with heat and sunlight and also, her mouse. She pulled up her email and then sat back with her mug in hand and watched seventeen drop into her box before she heard the whine of the screen door. She squinted at the time display in the top right corner of her screen (She'd left her damned glasses upstairs; what the hell? Was she losing her mind?) and wondered who was coming inside at twenty after five in the morning.

She drew her legs up to rest her feet on the edge of her chair— something she did often while thinking at her Mac—and turned curious eyes to the back door across the kitchen. She sipped her coffee and listened to the doorknob turn and then the last tiny whine of the screen closing and the bump of the back door against the wall, because no matter how you prepared for it, the door always got away from you and bumped the wall. There was even a half moon chunk taken out of the wall where the top of the knob banged it consistently.

Ingrid had been prepared to watch her baby sister sneak in, maybe even in the clothes she'd been wearing the night before. After all, Amber Williams was no stranger to the walk of shame. It wasn't Amber that tread silently into the kitchen, though. It was Hadley, Amber's fourteen-year-old daughter. Ingrid swallowed her shock with a mouthful of hot coffee and then wished she wouldn't have, because not only did it burn her tongue, but also it would make her sick before it was over.

No matter what Hadley had been doing, Ingrid doubted she'd tell Amber. Sure, she thought her sister should know that her fourteen-year-old kid was sneaking out. But as she hadn't seen or talked to Amber in a few years before this week, she figured it wasn't really her place.

Ingrid hadn't been an angel when she was fourteen, but she was pretty sure she hadn't started sneaking out of the house until she was at least sixteen. Besides, when she snuck out of the house, it was to meet Scott, and he was harmless. *Well.* Maybe, maybe not. He'd married her. But probably a year of marriage didn't really count for anything.

Hadley still hadn't noticed Ingrid at the table, even though the gray was now shot through with the spooky glow of a computer screen in the dark. Ingrid watched her shake her long dark hair out and then unzip her coat. She didn't appear to be drunk: no stumbling or drunk walking, where you're trying really hard to convince everyone, including yourself, that you aren't drunk.

Why sneak out if you aren't drinking? Was she meeting a boy? *Seriously?* At *sixteen*, Ingrid had been into only boys that you'd find on posters and album covers. Andy Gibb. Shaun Cassidy. She hadn't really known then that boys, *real boys*, existed, outside of the mean and often obnoxious boys she'd gone to school with.

"Aunt Ingrid." Hadley jumped, and Ingrid almost jumped too, and that would have been disastrous. She'd rather not start her day with a hot coffee shower. Instead, she took a drink and watched Hadley over her mug and raised her eyebrows as the young girl tugged her boots off—Seriously? There was a rug just inside the door, where Hadley could have removed her boots without tracking shit across the tile floor— and approached the table with reluctance that almost made Ingrid smile.

"Cold out there?" Ingrid's voice was a little sharp in the gray room, but as she hadn't spoken out loud yet this morning, the dregs of sleep sort of softened it.

"Um." Hadley nodded enthusiastically. Even in the semidarkness, Ingrid could see her eyes sparkle, could make out the thick fringe of her eyelashes. Hadley Williams was every bit the beauty her mother had been as a teenager. Ingrid wondered if Amber was going to watch her own mistakes play out with her daughter in the starring role.

"Want some coffee?" Ingrid offered, though she figured Hadley would turn her down and probably roll her eyes. To her surprise, Hadley shot a look at the coffeemaker and made a beeline for it. Desperate for coffee or desperate to get away from Ingrid?

Her laptop dinged and drew her attention away from her niece. Over two hundred email. She sighed and scanned the list, recognizing some addresses. Clueless on others. Most of them, actually. She took another drink of her coffee, lowered her feet to the floor and started clicking through her new mail. Normally, she loved email from readers, but now wasn't a good time for it.

"Are you gonna tell my mom?" Hadley asked as she joined Ingrid at the table.

Ingrid looked up from the glowing screen and blinked at her niece. Wished she had her damned glasses, because reading from her computer without them was sure to bring on a hellacious headache. Before she could answer, bright yellow light flooded the kitchen, and Ingrid held her breath.

"Tell your mom what?"

***

Also by Tracy Broemmer

Women's Fiction Novels:

Luther's Cross: 10th Anniversary Edition

Just Like Them

Small Hours

Two Story Home

Say Everything

Sketching Litchfield Lake

Damsel

Truth Is, The Williams Legacy, Book 1

Other People's Ugly, The Williams Legacy, Book 2

Omissions, The Williams Legacy, Book 3

Currently Out of Print:

Every Little Thing, Lorelei Bluffs, Book 1

Two A.M., Lorelei Bluffs, Book 2

Blind, Lorelei Bluffs, Book 3

Leaving July, Lorelei Bluffs, Book 4

Hesitation Marks, Lorelei Bluffs, Book 5

Four Letter Words, Lorelei Bluffs, Book 6

See Kate, Lorelei Bluffs, Book 7

Loved You More, Lorelei Bluffs, Book 8

A Lorelei Ending, Lorelei Bluffs, Book 9

I Do, Lorelei Bluffs, Book 10

Come Home for Christmas

About the Author

Tracy Broemmer is the author of several contemporary romance novels including the 515 Whiskey Series, Shameless Santa, and the Mississippi Queen Trilogy. Tracy also writes women's fiction and is the author of the Williams Legacy series as well as several stand-alone titles.

Tracy's books have been called gripping, emotional, and timely, and readers describe her characters as real and relatable

Tracy lives in Midwestern Illinois with her husband of 32 years. For a full backlist of titles, visit her on the web at www.broemmerbooks.com

Sign up for her newsletter at the bottom of the home page.